AMERICAN GHOSTS AND OLD WORLD WONDERS

Angela Carter was born in 1940. She read English at Bristol University, and from 1976–8 was fellow in Creative Writing at Sheffield University. She lived in Japan, the United States and Australia. Her first novel *Shadow Dance*, was published in 1965, followed by *The Magic Toyshop* (1967, John Llewellyn Rhys Prize), *Several Perceptions* (1968, Somerset Maugham Award), *Heroes And Villains* (1969), *Love* (1971), *The Passion Of New Eve* (1977), *Nights At The Circus* (1984, James Tait Black Memorial Prize) and *Wise Children* (1991). She published two previous collections of short stories, *Fireworks* (1974) and *The Bloody Chamber* (1979, Cheltenham Festival of Literature Award). She was the author of *The Sadeian Woman: An Exercise In Cultural History* (1979), and two collections of journalism, *Nothing Sacred* (1982) and *Expletives Deleted* (1992). She died in February 1992.

BY ANGELA CARTER

Fiction

Shadow Dance
The Magic Toyshop
Several Perceptions
Heroes And Villains
Love
The Infernal Desire Machines Of Dr Hoffman
Fireworks
The Passion Of New Eve
The Bloody Chamber
Nights At The Circus
Wise Children
American Ghosts And Old World Wonders

Non-Fiction

The Sadeian Woman: An Exercise In Cultural History
Nothing Sacred: Selected Writings
The Virago Book Of Fairytales (editor)
Expletives Deleted

Angela Carter

AMERICAN GHOSTS AND OLD WORLD WONDERS

VINTAGE

VINTAGE
20 Vauxhall Bridge Road, London SW1V 2SA

London Melbourne Sydney Auckland Johannesburg
and agencies throughout the world

First published by Chatto & Windus Ltd, 1993

Vintage edition 1994

2 4 6 8 10 9 7 5 3 1

Printed and bound in Great Britain by
Cox & Wyman, Reading, Berkshire

ISBN 0 09 913371 7

Contents

Acknowledgements

A version of 'Lizzie's Tiger' ws first published in *Cosmopolitan* (September 1991) and broadcast on Radio 3. 'John Ford's *'Tis Pity She's a Whore'* appeared in *Granta 25* (Autumn 1988), a version of 'The Merchant of Shadows' in the *London Review of Books* (26 October 1989) and 'In Pantoland' in *The Guardian* (24 December 1991). 'Ashputtle *or* The Mother's Ghost' was first published in the *Virago Book of Ghost Stories* (Virago, 1987), and a shorter version was published in *Soho Square* (Bloomsbury, 1991). A version of 'Impressions: The Wrightsman Magdalene' appeared in *FMR Magazine* (February 1992).

Introduction

When Angela Carter died from lung cancer in February 1992, her directions to those dealing with her literary estate were expansive. Her agent, her publisher and her literary executor (me) were to do 'anything to make money for my boys' – her husband Mark and son Alexander. No vulgarity was to be spared; any one of her fifteen books could be set to music or acted on ice. She also left particular notes about two books she hoped would be published soon. One was *The Second Virago Book of Fairy Tales*, which she had compiled and for which she had prepared half the notes. The other was to contain seven stories: 'all together, these *might* make a slim combined volume, to be called *American Ghosts and Old World Wonders*.'

She was anxious about the length – the sheet on which she listed the stories is decorated with word-counts and sums – but she was, as usual, completely confident about the material and its arrangement. These stories, written late in Angela's life, are about legends and myths and marvels, about Wild Western girls and pagan practices. They divide between Europe and America and between old and new ways of story-telling and celebration: Angela enjoyed carnival in different forms, as music hall or pantomime and as film – 'I like,' she said, 'anything that flickers.' Several further uncollected pieces were discovered after her death and considered for this book. Two were included: 'Gun for the Devil', an unfinished draft for a screenplay, attached itself naturally by form and content to the more polished and punning 'John Ford's *'Tis Pity She's a Whore'*; it also has things to say about the New World being not so new. 'The Ghost Ships', running with its magical cargo between the Old World and the New, bridged the two sections. Other items – written for page, screen or stage over the years – will be published later.

The pieces appear here as they were published in various magazines, with one or two exceptions. The Mary Magdalene story incorporates some additions Angela made to the text after it had been published: notably a new opening sentence, which provides a less stately beginning, and, in the first half, a few typical wrynesses – 'self-punishment is its own reward,' for example. (On the other hand, a scribbled instruction in the margins of this story to 'describe the picture' has been understood by the editors not as an authorial emendation but as Angela bullying herself.) A few Carteresque spellings have been brought into line with convention (at the risk in one instance of crushing a coinage – 'indistinguished'); one sentence, in 'Ashputtle', has been reworked because it lacked a main verb.

The preoccupations and style of these pieces give some glimmers of what Angela might have written next. They also contain a glimpse of an unachieved novel. When Angela died she left with her publishers the synopsis for a novel about Jane Eyre's step-daughter, *Adela*, but some years earlier she had had a different idea. She had wanted to write about the parent-killer Lizzie Borden. A story which appeared in the *London Review of Books* in 1981 under the title 'Mise-en-Scène for a Parricide' (later published in *Black Venus* as 'The Fall River Axe Murders') describes in scorching detail the day of the murder; 'Lizzie's Tiger', collected here, deals with events earlier in Lizzie's life. The stories are quite different; both are characteristic. Taken together, they show what a fine, fierce book we might have had.

SUSANNAH CLAPP

PART ONE

Lizzie's Tiger

When the circus came to town and Lizzie saw the tiger, they were living on Ferry Street, in a very poor way. It was the time of the greatest parsimony in their father's house; everyone knows the first hundred thousand is the most difficult and the dollar bills were breeding slowly, slowly, even if he practised a little touch of usury on the side to prick his cash in the direction of greater productivity. In another ten years' time, the War between the States would provide rich pickings for the coffin-makers, but, back then, back in the Fifties, well – if he had been a praying man, he would have gone down on his knees for a little outbreak of summer cholera or a touch, just a touch, of typhoid. To his chagrin, there had been nobody to bill when he had buried his wife.

For, at that time, the girls were just freshly orphaned. Emma was thirteen, Lizzie four – stern and square, a squat rectangle of a child. Emma parted Lizzie's hair in the middle, stretched it back over each side of her bulging forehead and braided it tight. Emma dressed her, undressed her, scrubbed her night and morning with a damp flannel, and humped the great lump of little girl around in her arms whenever Lizzie would let her, although Lizzie was not a demonstrative child and did not show affection easily, except to the head of the house, and then only when she wanted something. She knew where the power was and, intuitively feminine in spite of her gruff appearance, she knew how to court it.

3

That cottage on Ferry – very well, it was a slum; but the undertaker lived on unconcerned among the stiff furnishings of his defunct marriage. His bits and pieces would be admired today if they turned up freshly beeswaxed in an antique store, but in those days they were plain old-fashioned, and time would only make them more so in that dreary interior, the tiny house he never mended, eroding clapboard and diseased paint, mildew on the dark wallpaper with a brown pattern like brains, the ominous crimson border round the top of the walls, the sisters sleeping in one room in one thrifty bed.

On Ferry, in the worst part of town, among the dark-skinned Portuguese fresh off the boat with their earrings, flashing teeth and incomprehensible speech, come over the ocean to work the mills whose newly erected chimneys closed in every perspective; every year more chimneys, more smoke, more newcomers, and the peremptory shriek of the whistle that summoned to labour as bells had once summoned to prayer.

The hovel on Ferry stood, or, rather, leaned at a bibulous angle on a narrow street cut across at an oblique angle by another narrow street, all the old wooden homes like an upset cookie jar of broken gingerbread houses lurching this way and that way, and the shutters hanging off their hinges and windows stuffed with old newspapers, and the snagged picket fence and raised voices in unknown tongues and howling of dogs who, since puppyhood, had known of the world only the circumference of their chain. Outside the parlour window were nothing but rows of counterfeit houses that sometimes used to scream.

Such was the anxious architecture of the two girls' early childhood.

A hand came in the night and stuck a poster, showing the head of a tiger, on to a picket fence. As soon as Lizzie

4

saw the poster, she wanted to go to the circus, but Emma had no money, not a cent. The thirteen-year-old was keeping house at that time, the last skivvy just quit with bad words on both sides. Every morning, Father would compute the day's expenses, hand Emma just so much, no more. He was angry when he saw the poster on the fence; he thought the circus should have paid him rental for the use. He came home in the evening, sweet with embalming fluid, saw the poster, purpled with fury, ripped it off, tore it up.

Then it was suppertime. Emma was no great shakes at cookery and Father, dismissing the possibility of another costly skivvy until such time as plague struck, already pondered the cost-efficiency of remarriage; when Emma served up her hunks of cod, translucently uncooked within, her warmed-over coffee and a dank loaf of baker's bread, it almost put him in a courting mood, but that is not to say his meal improved his temper. So that, when his youngest climbed kitten-like upon his knee and, lisping, twining her tiny fingers in his gunmetal watch-chain, begged small change for the circus, he answered her with words of unusual harshness, for he truly loved this last daughter, whose obduracy recalled his own.

Emma unhandily darned a sock.

'Get that child to bed before I lose my temper!'

Emma dropped the sock and scooped up Lizzie, whose mouth set in dour lines of affront as she was borne off. The square-jawed scrap, deposited on the rustling straw mattress – oat straw, softest and cheapest – sat where she had been dropped and stared at the dust in a sunbeam. She seethed with resentment. It was moist midsummer, only six o'clock and still bright day outside.

She had a whim of iron, this one. She swung her feet on to the stool upon which the girls climbed down out of bed, thence to the floor. The kitchen door stood open for air behind the screen door. From the parlour came the low murmur of Emma's voice as she read *The Providence Journal* aloud to Father.

Next-door's lean and famished hound launched itself at the fence in a frenzy of yapping that concealed the creak of Lizzie's boots on the back porch. Unobserved, she was off – off and away! – trotting down Ferry Street, her cheeks pink with self-reliance and intent. She would not be denied. The circus! The word tinkled in her head with a red sound, as if it might signify a profane church.

'That's a tiger,' Emma had told her as, hand in hand, they inspected the poster on their fence.

'A tiger is a big cat,' Emma added instructively.

How big a cat?

A *very* big cat.

A dumpy, red-striped, regular cat of the small, domestic variety greeted Lizzie with a raucous mew from atop a gatepost as she stumped determinedly along Ferry Street; our cat, Ginger, whom Emma, in a small ecstasy of sentimental whimsy presaging that of her latter protracted spinsterhood, would sometimes call Miss Ginger, or even Miss Ginger Cuddles. Lizzie, however, sternly ignored Miss Ginger Cuddles. Miss Ginger Cuddles sneaked. The cat put out a paw as Lizzie brushed past, as if seeking to detain her, as if to suggest she took second thoughts as to her escapade, but, for all the apparent decision with which Lizzie put one firm foot before the other, she had not the least idea where the circus might be and would not have got there at all without the help of a gaggle of ragged Irish children from Corkey Row, who happened by in the company of a lean, black and tan, barking dog of unforeseen breed that had *this* much in common with Miss Ginger Cuddles, it could go whither it pleased.

This free-ranging dog with its easy-going grin took a fancy to Lizzie and, yapping with glee, danced around the little figure in the white pinafore as it marched along. Lizzie reached out to pat its head. She was a fearless girl.

The child-gang saw her pet their dog and took a fancy to her for the same reason as crows settle on one particular tree. Their wild smiles circled round her. 'Going to the circus, are ye? See the clown and the ladies dancing?' Lizzie knew nothing about clowns and dancers, but she nodded, and one boy took hold of one hand, another of the other, so they raced her off between them. They soon saw her little legs could not keep up their pace, so the ten-year-old put her up on his shoulders where she rode like a lord. Soon they came to a field on the edge of town.

'See the big top?' There was a red and white striped tent of scarcely imaginable proportions, into which you could have popped the entire house on Ferry, and the yard too, with enough room to spare inside for another house, and another — a vast red and white striped tent, with ripping naphtha flares outside and, besides this, all manner of other tents, booths and stalls, dotted about the field, but most of all she was impressed by the great number of people, for it seemed to her that the whole town must be out tonight, yet, when they looked closely at the throng, nowhere at all was anyone who looked like she did, or her father did, or Emma; nowhere that old New England lantern jaw, those ice-blue eyes.

She was a stranger among these strangers, for all here were those the mills had brought to town, the ones with different faces. The plump, pink-cheeked Lancashire mill-hands, with brave red neckerchiefs; the sombre features of the Canucks imbibing fun with characteristic gloom; and the white smiles of the Portuguese, who knew how to enjoy themselves, laughter tripping off their tipsy-sounding tongues.

'Here y'are!' announced her random companions as they dumped her down and, feeling they had amply done their duty by their self-imposed charge, they capered off among the throng, planning, perhaps, to slither under the canvas and so enjoy the shows for free, or even to pick a pocket or two to complete the treat, who knows?

Above the field, the sky now acquired the melting tones of the end of the day, the plush, smoky sunsets unique to these unprecedented industrial cities, sunsets never seen in this world before the Age of Steam that set the mills in motion that made us all modern.

At sunset, the incomparably grave and massive light of New England acquires a monumental, a Roman sensuality; under this sternly voluptuous sky, Lizzie abandoned herself to the unpremeditated smells and never-before-heard noises – hot fat in a vat of frying doughnuts; horse-dung; boiling sugar; frying onions; popping corn; freshly churned earth; vomit; sweat; cries of vendors; crack of rifles from the range; singsong of the white-faced clown, who clattered a banjo, while a woman in pink fleshings danced upon a little stage. Too much for Lizzie to take in at once, too much for Lizzie to take in at all – too rich a feast for her senses, so that she was taken a little beyond herself and felt her head spinning, a vertigo, a sense of profound strangeness overcoming her.

All unnoticeably small as she was, she was taken up by the crowd and tossed about among insensitive shoes and petticoats, too close to the ground to see much else for long; she imbibed the frenetic bustle of the midway through her nose, her ears, her skin that twitched, prickled, heated up with excitement so that she began to colour up in the way she had, her cheeks marked with red, like the marbling on the insides of the family Bible. She found herself swept by the tide of the crowd to a long table where hard cider was sold from a barrel.

The white tablecloth was wet and sticky with spillage and gave forth a dizzy, sweet, metallic odour. An old woman filled tin mugs at the barrel spigot, mug after mug, and threw coins on to other coins into a tin box – splash, chink, clang. Lizzie clung on to the edge of the table to prevent herself being carried away again. Splash, chink, clang. Trade was brisk, so the old woman never turned the spigot off and cider cascaded on to the ground on the other side of the table.

The devil got into Lizzie, then. She ducked down and sneaked in under the edge of the tablecloth, to hide in the resonant darkness and crouch on the crushed grass in fresh mud, as she held out her unobserved hands under the discontinuous stream from the spigot until she collected two hollowed palmfuls, which she licked up, and smacked her lips. Filled, licked, smacked again. She was so preoccupied with her delicious thievery that she jumped half out of her skin when she felt a living, quivering thing thrust into her neck in that very sensitive spot where her braids divided. Something moist and intimate shoved inquisitively at the nape of her neck.

She craned round and came face to face with a melancholy piglet, decently dressed in a slightly soiled ruff. She courteously filled her palms with cider and offered it to her new acquaintance, who sucked it up eagerly. She squirmed to feel the wet quiver of the pig's curious lips against her hands. It drank, tossed its pink snout, and trotted off out the back way from the table.

Lizzie did not hesitate. She followed the piglet past the dried-cod smell of the cider-seller's skirts. The piglet's tail disappeared beneath a cart piled with fresh barrels that was

9

pulled up behind the stall. Lizzie pursued the engaging piglet to find herself suddenly out in the open again, but this time in an abrupt margin of pitch black and silence. She had slipped out of the circus grounds through a hole in their periphery, and the dark had formed into a huge clot, the night, whilst Lizzie was underneath the table; behind her were the lights, but here only shadowy undergrowth, stirring, and then the call of a night bird.

The pig paused to rootle the earth, but when Lizzie reached out to stroke it, it shook its ears out of its eyes and took off at a great pace into the countryside. However, her attention was immediately diverted from this disappointment by the sight of a man who stood with his back to the lights, leaning slightly forward. The cider-barrel-spigot sound repeated itself. Fumbling with the front of his trousers, he turned round and tripped over Lizzie, because he was a little unsteady on his feet and she was scarcely to be seen among the shadows. He bent down and took hold of her shoulders.

'Small child,' he said, and belched a puff of acridity into her face. Lurching a little, he squatted right down in front of her, so they were on the same level. It was so dark that she could see of his face only the hint of a moustache above the pale half-moon of his smile.

'Small girl,' he corrected himself, after a closer look. He did not speak like ordinary folks. He was not from around these parts. He belched again, and again tugged at his trousers. He took firm hold of her right hand and brought it tenderly up between his squatting thighs.

'Small girl, do you know what *this* is for?'

She felt buttons; serge; something hairy; something moist and moving. She didn't mind it. He kept his hand on hers and made her rub him for a minute or two. He hissed between his teeth: 'Kissy, kissy from Missy?'

She *did* mind that and shook an obdurate head; she did not like her father's hard, dry, imperative kisses, and endured them only for the sake of power. Sometimes Emma touched her cheek lightly with unparted lips. Lizzie would allow no more. The man sighed when she shook her head, took her hand away from his crotch, softly folded it up on its fingers and gave her hand ceremoniously back to her.

'Gratuity,' he said, felt in his pocket and flipped her a nickel. Then he straightened up and walked away. Lizzie put the coin in her pinafore pocket and, after a moment's thought, stumped off after the funny man along the still, secret edges of the field, curious as to what he might do next.

But now surprises were going on all round her in the bushes, mewings, squeaks, rustlings, although the funny man paid no attention to them, not even when a stately fat woman rose up under his feet, huge as a moon and stark but for her stays, but for black cotton stockings held up by garters with silk rosettes on them, but for a majestic hat of black leghorn with feathers. The woman addressed the drunken man angrily, in a language with a good many k's in it, but he ploughed on indifferently and Lizzie scuttled unseen after, casting an inquisitive backward glance. She had never seen a woman's naked breasts since she could remember, and this pair of melons jiggled entrancingly as the fat woman shook her fist in the wake of the funny man before she parted her thighs with a wet smack and sank down on her knees again in the grass in which something unseen moaned.

Then a person scarcely as tall as Lizzie herself, dressed up like a little drummer-boy, somersaulted – head over heels – directly across their paths, muttering to himself as he did so. Lizzie had just the time to see that, although he was small, he was not shaped quite right, for his head seemed to have been pressed into his shoulders with some violence, but then he was gone.

Don't think any of this frightened her. She was not the kind of child that frightens easily.

Then they were at the back of a tent, not the big, striped tent, but another, smaller tent, where the funny man fumbled with the flap much as he had fumbled with his trousers. A bright mauve, ammoniac reek pulsed out from this tent; it was lit up inside like a Chinese lantern and glowed. At last he managed to unfasten and went inside. He did not so much as attempt to close up after him; he seemed to be in as great a hurry as the tumbling dwarf, so she slipped through too, but as soon as she was inside, she lost him, because there were so many other people there.

Feet of customers had worn all the grass from the ground and it had been replaced by sawdust, which soon stuck all over the mudpie Lizzie had become. The tent was lined with cages on wheels, but she could not see high enough to see what was inside them, yet, mixed with the everyday chatter around her, she heard strange cries that did not come from human throats, so she knew she was on the right track.

She saw what could be seen: a young couple, arm in arm, he whispering in her ear, she giggling; a group of three grinning, gaping youths, poking sticks within the bars; a family that went down in steps of size, a man, a woman, a boy, a girl, a boy, a girl, a boy, a girl, down to a baby of indeterminate sex in the woman's arms. There were many more present, but these were the people she took account of.

The gagging stench was worse than a summer privy and a savage hullabaloo went on all the time, a roaring as if the sea had teeth.

She eeled her way past skirts and trousers and scratched, bare legs of summer boys until she was standing beside the biggest brother of the staircase family at the front of the crowd, but still she could not see the tiger, even if she stood on tiptoe, she saw only wheels and the red and gold base of the cage, whereon was depicted a woman without any clothes, much like the one in the grass outside only without the hat and stockings, and some foliage, with a gilded moon and stars. The brother of the staircase family was much older than she, perhaps twelve, and clearly of the lower class, but clean and respectable-looking, although the entire family possessed that pale, peculiar look characteristic of the mill operatives. The brother looked down and saw a small child in a filthy pinafore peering and straining upwards.

'*Veux-tu voir le grand chat, ma petite?*'

Lizzie did not understand what he said, but she knew what he was saying and nodded assent. Mother looked over the head of the good baby in the lace bonnet as her son heaved Lizzie up in his arms for a good look.

'*Les poux . . .*' she warned, but her son paid her no heed.

'*Voilà, ma petite!*'

The tiger walked up and down, up and down; it walked up and down like Satan walking about the world and it burned. It burned so brightly, she was scorched. Its tail, thick as her father's forearm, twitched back and forth at the tip. The quick, loping stride of the caged tiger; its eyes like yellow coins of a foreign currency; its round, innocent, toy-like ears; the stiff whiskers sticking out with an artificial look; the red mouth from which the bright noise came. It walked up and down on straw strewn with bloody bones.

The tiger kept its head down, questing hither and thither though in quest of what might not be told. All its motion was slung from the marvellous haunches it held so high you could have rolled a marble down its back, if it would have let you, and the marble would have run down an oblique angle until it rolled over the domed forehead on to the floor. In its hind legs the tense muscles keened and sang. It was a miracle of dynamic suspension. It reached one end of the cage in a few paces and whirled around upon itself in one liquid motion; nothing could be quicker or more beautiful than its walk. It was all raw, vivid, exasperated nerves. Upon its pelt it bore the imprint of the bars behind which it lived.

The young lad who kept hold of her clung tight as she lunged forward towards the beast, but he could not stop her clutching the bars of the cage with her little fingers and he tried but he could not dislodge them. The tiger stopped in its track halfway through its mysterious patrol and looked at her. Her pale-blue Calvinist eyes of New England encountered with a shock the flat, mineral eyes of the tiger.

It seemed to Lizzie that they exchanged this cool regard for an endless time, the tiger and herself.

Then something strange happened. The svelte beast fell to its knees. It was as if it had been subdued by the presence of this child, as if this little child of all the children in the world, might lead it towards a peaceable kingdom where it need not eat meat. But only 'as if'. All we could see was, it knelt. A crackle of shock ran through the tent; the tiger was acting out of character.

Its mind remained, however, a law unto itself. We did not know what it was thinking. How could we?

It stopped roaring. Instead it started to emit a rattling purr. Time somersaulted. Space diminished to the field of attractive force between the child and the tiger. All that existed in the whole world now were Lizzie and the tiger.

Then, oh! then . . . it came towards her, as if she were winding it to her on an invisible string by the exercise of pure will. I cannot tell you how much she loved the tiger, nor how wonderful she thought it was. It was the power of her love that forced it to come to her, on its knees, like a penitent. It dragged its pale belly across the dirty straw towards the bars where the little soft creature hung by its hooked fingers. Behind it followed the serpentine length of its ceaselessly twitching tail.

There was a wrinkle in its nose and it buzzed and rumbled and they never took their eyes off one another, though neither had the least idea what the other meant.

The boy holding Lizzie got scared and pummelled her little fists, but she would not let go a grip as tight and senseless as that of the newborn.

Crack! The spell broke.

The world bounded into the ring.

A lash cracked round the tiger's carnivorous head, and a glorious hero sprang into the cage brandishing in the hand that did not hold the whip a three-legged stool. He wore fawn breeches, black boots, a bright red jacket frogged with gold, a tall hat. A dervish, he; he beckoned, crouched, pointed with the whip, menaced with the stool, leaped and twirled in a brilliant ballet of mimic ferocity, the dance of the Taming of the Tiger, to whom the tamer gave no chance to fight at all.

The great cat unpeeled its eyes off Lizzie's in a trice, rose up on its hind legs and feinted at the whip like our puss Ginger feints at a piece of paper dangled from a string. It batted at the tamer with its enormous paws, but the whip continued to confuse, irritate and torment it and, what with the shouting, the sudden, excited baying of the crowd, the dreadful confusion of the signs surrounding it, habitual custom, a lifetime's training, the tiger whimpered, laid back its ears and scampered away from the whirling man to an obscure corner of the stage, there to cower, while its flanks heaved, the picture of humiliation.

Lizzie let go of the bars and clung, mudstains and all, to her young protector for comfort. She was shaken to the roots by the attack of the trainer upon the tiger and her four-year-old roots were very near the surface.

The tamer gave his whip a final, contemptuous ripple around his adversary's whiskers that made it sink its huge head on the floor. Then he placed one booted foot on the tiger's skull and cleared his throat for speech. He was a hero. He was a tiger himself, but even more so, because he was a man.

'Ladies and gentlemen, boys and girls, this incomparable TIGER known as the Scourge of Bengal, and brought alive-oh to Boston from its native jungle but three short months before this present time, now, at my imperious command, offers you a perfect imitation of docility and obedience. But do not let the brute deceive you. Brute it was, and brute it remains. Not for nothing did it receive the soubriquet of Scourge for, in its native habitat, it thought nothing of consuming a dozen brown-skinned heathen for its breakfast and following up with a couple of dozen more for dinner!'

A pleasing shudder tingled through the crowd.

'This tiger,' and the beast whickered ingratiatingly when he named it, 'is the veritable incarnation of blood lust and fury; in a single instant, it can turn from furry quiescence into three hundred pounds, yes, three hundred POUNDS of death-dealing fury.

'The tiger is the cat's revenge.'

Oh, Miss Ginger, Miss Ginger Cuddles, who sat mewing censoriously on the gatepost as Lizzie passed by; who would have thought you seethed with such resentment!

The man's voice dropped to a confidential whisper and Lizzie, although she was in such a state, such nerves, recognised this was the same man as the one she had met behind the cider stall, although now he exhibited such erect mastery, not a single person in the tent would have thought he had been drinking.

'What is the nature of the bond between us, between the Beast and Man? Let me tell you. It is fear. Fear! Nothing but fear. Do you know how insomnia is the plague of the tamer of cats? How all night long, every night, we pace our quarters, impossible to close our eyes for brooding on what day, what hour, what moment the fatal beast will choose to strike?

'Don't think I cannot bleed, or that they have not wounded me. Under my clothes, my body is a palimpsest of scars, scar upon scar. I heal only to be once more broken open. No skin of mine that is not scar tissue. And I am always afraid, always; all the time in the ring, in the cage, now, this moment – this very moment, boys and girls, ladies and gentlemen, you see before you a man in the grip of mortal fear.

'Here and now I am in terror of my life.

'At this moment I am in this cage within a perfect death trap.'

Theatrical pause.

'But,' and here he knocked the tiger's nose with his whip-stock, so that it howled with pain and affront, 'but . . .' and Lizzie saw the secret frog he kept within his trousers shift a little, ' . . . BUT I'm not half so scared of the big brute as it is of me!'

He showed his red maw in a laugh.

'For I bring to bear upon its killer instinct a rational man's knowledge of the power of fear. The whip, the stool, are instruments of bluff with which I create his fear in my arena. In my cage, among my cats, I have established a hierarchy of FEAR and among my cats you might well say

I am TOP DOG, because I know that all the time they want to kill me, that is their project, that is their intention . . . but as for them, they just don't know what I might do next. No, sir!'

As if enchanted by the notion, he laughed out loud again, but by now the tiger, perhaps incensed by the unexpected blow on the nose, rumbled out a clear and incontrovertible message of disaffection and, with a quick jerk of its sculptured head, flung the man's foot away so that, caught off-balance, he half toppled over. And then the tiger was no longer a thing of stillness, of hard edges and clear outlines, but a whizz of black and red, maw and canines, in the air. On him.

The crowd immediately bayed.

But the tamer, with enormous presence of mind, seeing as how he was drunk, and, in the circumstances, with almost uncanny physical agility, bounced backwards on his boot-heels and thrust the stool he carried in his left hand into the fierce tiger's jaws, leaving the tiger worrying, gnawing, destroying the harmless thing, as a ragged black boy quickly unlatched the cage door and out the tamer leaped, unscathed, amidst hurrahs.

Lizzie's stunned little face was now mottled all over with a curious reddish-purple, with the heat of the tent, with passion, with the sudden access of enlightenment.

To see the rest of the stupendous cat act, the audience would have had to buy another ticket for the Big Top, besides the ticket for the menagerie, for which it had already paid, so, reluctant on the whole to do that, in spite of the promise of clowns and dancing ladies, it soon got bored with watching the tiger splintering the wooden stool, and drifted off.

'*Eh bien, ma petite,*' said her boy-nurse to her in a sweet, singsong, crooning voice. '*Tu as vu la bête! La bête du cauchemar!*'

The baby in the lace bonnet had slept peacefully through all this, but now began to stir and mumble. Its mother nudged her husband with her elbow.

'*On va, Papa?*'

The crooning, smiling boy brought his bright pink lips down on Lizzie's forehead for a farewell kiss. She could not bear that; she struggled furiously and shouted to be put down. With that, her cover broke and she burst out of her disguise of dirt and silence; half the remaining gawpers in the tent had kin been bleakly buried by her father, the rest owed him money. She was the most famous daughter in all Fall River.

'Well, if it ain't Andrew Borden's little girl! What are they Canucks doing with little Lizzie Borden?'

John Ford's
'Tis Pity She's a Whore

There was a rancher had two children, a son and then a daughter. A while after that, his wife died and was buried under two sticks nailed together to make a cross because there was no time, yet, to carve a stone.

Did she die of the loneliness of the prairies? Or was it anguish that killed her, anguish, and nostalgia for the close, warm, neighbourly life she had left behind her when she came to this emptiness? Neither. She died of the pressure of that vast sky, that weighed down upon her and crushed her lungs until she could not breathe any more, as if the prairies were the bedrock of an ocean in which she drowned.

She told her boy: 'Look after your sister.' He, blond, solemn, little; he and Death sat with her in the room of logs her husband split to build. Death, with high cheek-bones, wore his hair in braids. His invisible presence in the cabin mocked the existence of the cabin. The round-eyed boy clutched his mother's dry hand. The girl was younger.

NOTE:

John Ford (1586 *c.* 1639). English dramatist of the Jacobean period. His tragedy, *'Tis Pity She's a Whore*, was published in 1633. 'Deep in a dump John Ford alone was got/With folded arms and melancholy hat.' (*Choice Drollery*, 1656.)

John Ford (1895–1973). American film-maker. Filmography includes: *Stagecoach* (1938); *My Darling Clementine* (1946); *She Wore a Yellow Ribbon* (1949). 'My name is John Ford. I make Westerns.' (*John Ford*, Andrew Sinclair, New York 1979.)

Then the mother lay with the prairies and all that careless sky upon her breast, and the children lived in their father's house. So they grew up. In his spare time the rancher chiselled at a rock: 'Beloved wife of ... mother of ...' beneath the space at the top he had left for his own name.

America begins and ends in the cold and solitude. Up here, she pillows her head upon the Arctic snow. Down there, she dips her feet in the chilly waters of the South Atlantic, home of the perpetually restless albatross. America, with her torso of a woman at the time of this story, a woman with an hour-glass waist, a waist laced so tightly it snapped in two, and we put a belt of water there. America, with your child-bearing hips and your crotch of jungle, your swelling bosom of a nursing mother and your cold head, your cold head.

Its central paradox resides in this: that the top half doesn't know what the bottom half is doing. When I say the two children of the prairie, suckled on those green breasts, were the pure children of the continent, you know at once that they were *norteamericanos*, or I would not speak of them in the English language, which was their language, the language that silences the babble of this continent's multitude of tongues.

Blond children with broad, freckled faces, the boy in dungarees and the little girl in gingham and sunbonnet. In the old play, one John Ford called them Giovanni and Annabella; the other John Ford, in the movie, might call them Johnny and Annie-Belle.

Annie-Belle will bake bread, tramp the linen clean and cook the beans and bacon; this lily of the West had not spare time enough to pause and consider the lilies of the field, who never do a hand's turn. No, sir. A woman's work is never done and she became a woman early.

The gaunt paterfamilias would drive them into town to church on Sundays with the black Bible on his knee wherein their names and dates of birth were inscribed. In the buggy, his shy, big-boned, tow-headed son in best, dark, Sunday clothes, and Annie-Belle, at thirteen, fourteen, increasingly astonished at and rendered shy by her own lonely flowering. Fifteen. How pretty she was growing! They came to pray in God's house that, like their own, was built of split logs. Annie-Belle kept her eyes down; she was a good girl. They were good children. The widower drank, sometimes, but not much. They grew up in silence, in the enormous silence of the empty land, the silence that swallowed up the Saturday-night fiddler's tune, mocked the rare laughter at weddings and christenings, echoed, a vast margin, around the sermons of the preacher.

Silence and space and an unimaginable freedom which they dare not imagine.

Since his wife died, the rancher spoke rarely. They lived far out of town. He had no time for barn-raisings and church suppers. If she had lived, everything would have been different, but he occupied his spare moments in chiselling her gravestone. They did not celebrate Thanksgiving for he had nothing for which to give thanks. It was a hard life.

The Minister's wife made sure Annie-Belle knew a thing or two when she judged it about the time the girl's bleeding started. The Minister's wife, in a vague, pastoral way, thought about a husband for Annie-Belle, a wife for Johnny. 'Out there, in that little house on the prairie, so lonesome ... Nobody for those young folks to talk to 'cept cows, cows, cows.'

*

What did the girl think? In summer, of the heat, and how to keep flies out of the butter; in winter, of the cold. I do not know what else she thought. Perhaps, as young girls do, she thought that a stranger would come to town and take her away to the city and so on, but, since her imagination began and ended with her experience, the farm, work, the seasons, I think she did not think so far, as if she knew already she was the object of the object of her own desire for, in the bright light of the New World, nothing is obscure. But when they were children, all they knew was they loved each other just as, surely, a brother or a sister should.

She washed her hair in a tub. She washed her long, yellow hair. She was fifteen. It was spring. She washed her hair. It was the first time that year. She sat on the porch to dry her hair, she sat in the rocking-chair which her mother selected from the Sears' Roebuck catalogue, where her father would never sit, now. She propped a bit of mirror on the porch railing. It caught the sun and flashed. She combed out her wet hair in the mirror. There seemed to be an awful lot of it, tangling up the comb. She wore only her petticoat, the men were off with the cattle, nobody to see her pale shoulders except that Johnny came back. The horse threw him, he knocked his head against a stone. Giddy, he came back to the house, leading his pony, and she was busy untangling her hair and did not see him, nor have a chance to cover herself.

'Why, Johnny, I declare –'

Imagine an orchestra behind them: the frame house, the porch, the rocking-chair endlessly rocking, like a cradle, the white petticoat with eyelet lace, her water-darkened hair hanging on her shoulders and little trickles running down between her shallow breasts, the young man leading

23

the limping pony, and, inexhaustible as light, around them the tender land.

The 'Love Theme' swells and rises. She jumps up to tend him. The jogged mirror falls.

'Seven years' bad luck —'

In the fragments of the mirror, they kneel to see their round, blond, innocent faces that, superimposed upon one another, would fit at every feature, their faces, all at once the same face, the face that never existed until now, the pure face of America.

> EXTERIOR. PRAIRIE. DAY
> (Long shot) Farmhouse.
> (Close up) Petticoat falling on to porch of
>   farmhouse.

Wisconsin, Ohio, Iowa, Missouri, Kansas, Minnesota, Nebraska, the Dakotas, Wyoming, Montana . . . Oh, those enormous territories! That green vastness, in which anything is possible.

> EXTERIOR. PRAIRIE. DAY
> (Close up) Johnny and Annie-Belle kiss.
> 'Love Theme' up.
> Dissolve.

No. It wasn't like that! Not in the least like that.

He put out his hand and touched her wet hair. He was giddy.

Annabella: Methinks you are not well.
Giovanni: Here's none but you and I. I think you love me, sister.
Annabella: Yes, you know I do.

And they thought, then, that they should kill themselves, together now, before they did it; they remembered tumbling together in infancy, how their mother laughed to see their kisses, their embraces, when they were too young to know they should not do it, yet even in their loneliness on the enormous plain they knew they must not do it . . . do what? How did they know what to do? From watching the cows with the bull, the bitch with the dog, the hen with the cock. They were country children. Turning from the mirror, each saw the other's face as if it were their own.

[*Music plays.*]
Giovanni: Let not this music be a dream, ye gods.
　For pity's sake, I beg you!
[*She kneels.*]
Annabella: On my knees,
　Brother, even by our mother's dust, I charge you
　Do not betray me to your mirth or hate.
　Love me, or kill me, brother.
[*He kneels.*]
Giovanni: On my knees,
　Sister, even by our mother's dust, I charge you
　Do not betray me to your mirth or hate.
　Love me, or kill me, sister.

> EXTERIOR. FARMHOUSE PORCH. DAY
> Upset water-tub, spilling over discarded
> 　petticoat.
> Empty rocking-chair, rocking, rocking.

It is the boy – or young man, rather – who is the most mysterious to me. The eagerness with which he embraces his fate. I imagine him mute or well-nigh mute; he is the silent type, his voice creaks with disuse. He turns the soil, he breaks the wills of the beautiful horses, he milks the cows, he works the land, he toils and sweats. His work consists of the vague, undistinguished 'work' of such folks in the movies. No cowboy, he, roaming the plains. Where the father took root, so has the son, in the soil that was never before broken until now.

And I imagine him with an intelligence nourished only by the black book of the father, and hence cruelly circumscribed, yet dense with allusion, seeing himself as a kind of Adam and she his unavoidable and irreplaceable Eve, the unique companion of the wilderness, although by their toil he knows they do not live in Eden and of the precise nature of the forbidden thing he remains in doubt.

For surely it cannot be this? This bliss? Who could forbid such bliss!

Was it bliss for her, too? Or was there more of love than pleasure in it? 'Look after your sister.' But it was she who looked after him as soon as she knew how and pleasured him in the same spirit as she fed him.

Giovanni: I am lost forever.

Lost in the green wastes, where the pioneers were lost. Death with his high cheekbones and his braided hair helped Annie-Belle take off her clothes. She closed her eyes so that she could not see her own nakedness. Death showed her how to touch him and him her. There is more to it than farmyard ways.

> INTERIOR. MINISTER'S HOUSE. DAY
> Dinner-table. Minister's wife dishing portions
> from a pot for her husband and her son.

MINISTER'S WIFE: 'Tain't right, just ain't right, those two out there, growing up like savages, never seeing nobody.

MINISTER'S SON: She's terribly pretty, Mama.

The Minister's wife and the Minister turn to look at the young man. He blushes slowly but comprehensively.

The rancher knew nothing. He worked. He kept the iron core of grief within him rustless. He looked forward to his solitary, once-monthly drink, alone on the porch, and on those nights they took a chance and slept together in the log cabin under the patchwork quilt made in the 'log cabin' pattern by their mother. Each time they lay down there together, as if she obeyed a voice that came out of the quilt telling her to put the light out, she would extinguish the candle-flame between her fingertips. All around them, the tactility of the dark.

She pondered the irreversibility of defloration. According to what the Minister's wife said, she had lost everything and was a lost girl. And yet this change did not seem to have changed her. She turned to the only one she loved, and the desolating space around them diminished to that of the soft grave their bodies dented in the long grass by the creek. When winter came, they made quick, dangerous love among the lowing beasts in the barn. The snow melted and all was green enough to blind you and there was a vinegarish smell from the rising of the sharp juices of spring. The birds came back.

A dusk bird went chink-chink-chink like a single blow on the stone xylophone of the Chinese classical orchestra.

EXTERIOR. FARMHOUSE PORCH. DAY
Annie-Belle, in apron, comes out on
  homestead porch; strikes metal triangle.

ANNIE-BELLE: Dinner's ready!

INTERIOR. FARMHOUSE. NIGHT
Supper-table. Annie-Belle serves beans. None
  for herself.

JOHNNY: Annie-Belle, you're not eating
  anything tonight.

ANNIE-BELLE: Can't rightly fancy anything
  tonight.

The dusk bird went chink-chink-chink with the sound of a chisel on a gravestone.

He wanted to run away with her, west, further west, to Utah, to California where they could live as man and wife, but she said: 'What about Father? He's lost enough already.' When she said that, she put on, not his face, but that of their mother, and he knew in his bones the child inside her would part them.

The Minister's son, in his Sunday coat, came courting Annie-Belle. He is the second lead, you know in advance, from his tentative manner and mild eyes; he cannot long survive in this prairie scenario. He came courting Annie-Belle although his mother wanted him to go to college. 'What will you do at college with a young wife?' said his mother. But he put away his books; he took the buggy to go out and visit her. She was hanging washing out on the line.

Sound of the wind buffeting the sheets, the very sound of loneliness.

Soranzo: Have you not the will to love?
Annabella: Not you.
Soranzo: Who, then?
Annabella: That's as the fates infer.

She lowered her head and drew her foot back and forth in the dust. Her breasts hurt, she felt queasy.

> EXTERIOR. PRAIRIE. DAY
> Johnny and Annie-Belle walking on the
>   prairie.

> ANNIE-BELLE: I think he likes me, Johnny.

> Pan blue sky, with clouds. Johnny and Annie-
>   Belle, dwarfed by the landscape, hand in
>   hand, heads bowed. Their hands slowly
>   part.

> Now they walk with gradually increasing
>   distance between them.

The light, the unexhausted light of North America that, filtered through celluloid, will become the light by which we see America looking at itself.

Correction: will become the light by which we see *North* America looking at itself.

> EXTERIOR. FARMHOUSE PORCH. DAY
> Row of bottles on a fence.

Bang, bang, bang. Johnny shoots the bottles
    one by one.
Annie-Belle on porch, washing dishes in a tub.
Tears run down her face.

EXTERIOR. FARMHOUSE PORCH. DAY
Father on porch, feet up on railing, glass and
    bottle to hand.
Sun going down over prairies.
Bang, bang, bang.

(Father's point of view) Johnny shooting
    bottles off the fence.

Clink of father's bottle against glass.

EXTERIOR. FARMHOUSE. DAY
Minister's son rides along track in long shot.
    Bang, bang, bang.

Annie-Belle, clean dress, tidy hair, red eyes,
    comes out of house on to porch. Clink of
    father's bottle against glass.

EXTERIOR. FARMHOUSE. DAY
Minister's son tethers horse. He has brushed
    his Sunday coat. In his hand, a posy of
    flowers — cottage roses, sweetbrier, daisies.
    Annie-Belle smiles, takes posy.

ANNIE-BELLE: Oh!

Holds up pricked forefinger; blood drops on
    to a daisy.

MINISTER'S SON: Let me . . .

Takes her hand. Kisses the little wound.

. . . make it better.

Bang. Bang. Bang.
Clink of bottle on glass.

(Close up) Annie-Belle, smiling, breathing in
the scent from her posy.

And, perhaps, had it been possible, she would have learned
to love the Minister's gentle son before she married him,
but, not only was it impossible, she also carried within her
the child that meant she must be married quickly.

INTERIOR. CHURCH. DAY
Harmonium. Father and Johnny by the altar.
Johnny white, strained; father stoical.
Minister's wife thin-lipped, furious.
Minister's son and Annie-Belle, in simple
white cotton wedding-dress, join hands.

MINISTER: Do you take this woman . . .

(Close up) Minister's son's hand slipping
wedding ring on to Annie-Belle's finger.

INTERIOR. BARN. NIGHT
Fiddle and banjo old-time music.
Vigorous square dance going on; bride and
groom lead.

Father at table, glass in hand.
Johnny, beside him, reaching for bottle.

Bride and groom come together at end of
     dance; groom kisses bride's cheek. She
     laughs.

(Close up) Annie-Belle looking shyly up at the
     Minister's son.

The dance parts them again; as Annie-Belle is
     handed down the row of men, she staggers
     and faints.

Consternation.

Minister's son and Johnny both run towards
     her.

Johnny lifts her up in his arms, her head on
     his shoulder. Eyes opening. Minister's son
     reaches out for her. Johnny lets him take
     hold of her.

She gazes after Johnny beseechingly as he
     disappears among the crowd.

Silence swallowed up the music of the fiddle and the
banjo; Death with his hair in braids spread out the sheets
on the marriage bed.

> INTERIOR. MINISTER'S HOUSE. BEDROOM.
> NIGHT
> Annie-Belle in bed, in a white nightgown,

> clutching the pillow, weeping. Minister's
> son, bare back, sitting on side of bed with
> his back to camera, head in hands.

In the morning, her new mother-in-law heard her vomiting into the chamber pot and, in spite of her son's protests, stripped Annie-Belle and subjected her to a midwife's inspection. She judged her three months gone, or more. She dragged the girl round the room by the hair, slapped her, punched her, kicked her, but Annie-Belle would not tell the father's name, only promised, swore on the grave of her dead mother, that she would be a good girl in future. The young bridegroom was too bewildered by this turn of events to have an opinion about it; only, to his vague surprise, he knew he still loved the girl although she carried another man's child.

'Bitch! Whore!' said the Minister's wife and struck Annie-Belle a blow across the mouth that started her nose bleeding.

'Now, stop that, Mother,' said the gentle son. 'Can't you see she ain't well?'

The terrible day drew to its end. The mother-in-law would have thrown Annie-Belle out on the street, but the boy pleaded for her, and the Minister, praying for guidance, found himself opening the Bible at the parable of the woman taken in adultery and meditated well upon it.

'Only tell me the name of the father,' her young husband said to Annie-Belle.

'Better you don't know it,' she said. Then she lied: 'He's gone, now; gone out west.'

'Was it –?' naming one or two.

'You never knew him. He came by the ranch on his way out west.'

Then she burst out crying again, and he took her in his arms.

'It will be all over town,' said the mother-in-law. 'That girl made a fool of you!'

She slammed the dishes on the table and would have made the girl eat out the back door, but the young husband laid her a place at table with his own hands and led her in and sat her down in spite of his mother's black looks. They bowed their heads for grace. Surely, the Minister thought, seeing his boy cut bread for Annie-Belle and lay it on her plate, my son is a saint. He began to fear for him.

'I won't do anything unless you want,' her husband said in the dark after the candle went out.

The straw with which the mattress was stuffed rustled beneath her as she turned away from him.

INTERIOR. FARMHOUSE KITCHEN. NIGHT
Johnny comes in from outside, looks at father
    asleep in rocking-chair.
Picks up some discarded garment of Annie-
    Belle's from the back of a chair, buries
    face in it.
Shoulders shake.
Opens cupboard, takes out bottle.
Uncorks with teeth. Drinks.
Bottle in hand, goes out on porch.

EXTERIOR. PRAIRIE. NIGHT
(Johnny's point of view) Moon rising over
    prairie: the vast, the elegiac plain.
'Landscape Theme' rises.

INTERIOR. MINISTER'S SON'S ROOM. NIGHT
Annie-Belle and Minister's son in bed.

Moonlight through curtains. Both lie
there, open-eyed. Rustle of mattress.

ANNIE-BELLE: You awake?

Minister's son moves away from her.

ANNIE-BELLE: Reckon I never properly
knowed no young man before . . .

MINISTER'S SON: What about —

ANNIE-BELLE (shrugging the question off):
Oh . . .

Minister's son moves towards her.

For she did not consider her brother in this new category
of 'young men'; he was herself. So she and her husband
slept in one another's arms, that night, although they did
nothing else for she was scared it might harm the baby and
he was so full of pain and glory it was scarcely to be borne,
it was already enough, or too much, holding her tight, in
his terrible innocence.

It was not so much that she was pliant. Only, fearing the
worst, it turned out that the worst had already happened;
her sin found her out, or, rather, she found out she had
sinned only when he offered his forgiveness, and, from her
repentance, a new Annie-Belle sprang up, for whom the
past did not exist.

She would have said to him: 'It did not signify, my
darling; I only did it with my brother, we were alone
together under the vast sky that made us scared and so we
clung together and what happened, happened.' But she

35

knew she must not say that, that the most natural love of all was just precisely the one she must not acknowledge. To lie down on the prairie with a passing stranger was one thing. To lie down with her father's son was another. So she kept silent. And when she looked at her husband, she saw, not herself, but someone who might, in time, grow even more precious.

The next night, in spite of the baby, they did it, and his mother wanted to murder her and refused to get the breakfast for this prostitute, but Annie-Belle served them, put on an apron, cut the ham and cooked it, then scrubbed the floor with such humility, such evidence of gratitude that the older woman kept her mouth shut, her narrow lips tight as a trap, but she kept them shut for if there was one thing she feared, it was the atrocious gentleness of her menfolk. And. So.

Johnny came to the town, hungering after her; the gates of Paradise slammed shut in his face. He haunted the backyard of the Minister's house, hid in the sweetbrier, watched the candle in their room go out and still he could not imagine it, that she might do it with another man. But. She did.

At the store, all gossip ceased when she came in; all eyes turned towards her. The old men chewing tobacco spat brown streams when she walked past. The women's faces veiled with disapproval. She was so young, so unaccustomed to people. They talked, her husband and she; they would go, just go, out west, still further, west as far as the place where the ocean starts again, perhaps. With his schooling, he could get some clerking job or other. She would bear her child and he would love it. Then she would bear *their* children.

'Yes,' she said. 'We shall do that,' she said.

EXTERIOR. FARMHOUSE. DAY

Annie-Belle drives up in trap.

Johnny comes out on porch, in shirt-sleeves,
   bottle in hand.

Takes her reins. But she doesn't get down
   from the trap.

ANNIE-BELLE: Where's Daddy?

Johnny gestures towards the prairie.

ANNIE-BELLE (not looking at Johnny): Got
   something to tell him.

(Close up) Johnny.

JOHNNY: Ain't you got nothing to tell me?

(Close up) Annie-Belle.

ANNIE-BELLE: Reckon I ain't.

(Close-up) Johnny.

JOHNNY: Get down and visit a while, at least.

(Close-up) Annie-Belle.

ANNIE-BELLE: Can't hardly spare the time.

(Close up) Johnny and Annie-Belle.

JOHNNY: Got to scurry back, get your
   husband's dinner, is that it?

ANNIE-BELLE: Johnny . . . why haven't you
    come to church since I got married,
    Johnny?

Johnny shrugs, turns away.

EXTERIOR. FARMHOUSE. DAY
Annie-Belle gets down from trap, follows
    Johnny towards farmhouse.

ANNIE-BELLE: Oh, Johnny, you *knowed* we
    did wrong.

Johnny walks towards farmhouse.

ANNIE-BELLE: I count myself fortunate to
    have found forgiveness.

JOHNNY: What are you going to tell Daddy?

ANNIE-BELLE: I'm going out west.

Giovanni: What, chang'd so soon! hath your new sprightly
    lord
  Found out a trick in night-games more than we
  Could know in our simplicity? – Ha! is't so?
  Or does the fit come on you, to prove treacherous
  To your past vows and oaths?
Annabella: Why should you jest
  At my calamity.

EXTERIOR. FARMHOUSE. DAY

JOHNNY: Out west?

Annie-Belle nods.

JOHNNY: By yourself?

Annie-Belle shakes her head.

JOHNNY: With him?

Annie-Belle nods.
Johnny puts hand on porch rail, bends
    forward, hiding his face.

ANNIE-BELLE: It is for the best.

She puts her hand on his shoulder. He reaches
    out for her. She extricates herself. His
    hand, holding bottle; contents of bottle run
    out on grass.

ANNIE-BELLE: It was wrong, what we did.

JOHNNY: What about . . .

ANNIE-BELLE: It shouldn't ever have been
    made, poor little thing. You won't never
    see it. Forget everything. You'll find
    yourself a woman, you'll marry.

Johnny reaches out and clasps her roughly to
    him.

'No,' she said; 'never. No.' And fought and bit and scratched: 'Never! It's wrong. It's a sin.' But, worse than that, she said: 'I don't want to,' and she meant it, she knew she must not or else her new life, that lay before her, now, with the radiant simplicity of a child's drawing of a house, would be utterly destroyed. So she got free of him and ran to the buggy and drove back lickety-split to town, beating the pony round the head with the whip.

Accompanied by a black trunk like a coffin, the Minister and his wife drove with them to a railhead such as you have often seen on the movies – the same telegraph office, the same water-tower, the same old man with the green eyeshade selling tickets. Autumn was coming on. Annie-Belle could no longer conceal her pregnancy, out it stuck; her mother-in-law could not speak to her directly but addressed remarks through the Minister, who compensated for his wife's contempt by showing Annie-Belle all the honour due to a repentant sinner.

She wore a yellow ribbon. Her hair was long and yellow. The repentant harlot has the surprised look of a pregnant virgin.

She is pale. The pregnancy does not go well. She vomits all morning. She bleeds a little. Her husband holds her hand tight. Her father came last night to say goodbye to her; he looks older. He does not take care of himself. That Johnny did not come set the tongues wagging; the gossip is, he refuses to set eyes on his sister in her disgrace. That seems the only thing to explain his attitude. All know he takes no interest in girls himself.

'Bless you, children,' says the Minister. With that troubling air of incipient sainthood, the young husband settles

his wife down on the trunk and tucks a rug round her legs
for a snappy wind drives dust down the railroad track and
the hills are October mauve and brown. In the distance,
the train whistle blows, that haunting sound, blowing
across endless distance, the sound that underlines the
distance.

EXTERIOR. FARMHOUSE. DAY
Johnny mounts horse. Slings rifle over
    shoulder.
Kicks horse's sides.

EXTERIOR. RAILROAD. DAY
Train whistle. Burst of smoke.
Engine pulling train across prairie.

EXTERIOR. PRAIRIE. DAY
Johnny galloping down track.

EXTERIOR. RAILROAD. DAY
Train wheels turning.

EXTERIOR. PRAIRIE. DAY
Hooves churning dust.

EXTERIOR. STATION. DAY

MINISTER'S WIFE: Now, you take care of
    yourself, you hear? And – (but she can't
    bring herself to say it).

MINISTER: Be sure to tell us about the baby
    as soon as it comes.

> (Close up) Annie-Belle smiling gratefully.
> Train whistle.

And see them, now, as if posing for the photographer, the young man and the pregnant woman, sitting on a trunk, waiting to be transported onwards, away, elsewhere, she with the future in her belly.

> EXTERIOR. STATION. DAY
> Station master comes out of ticket-office.
>
> STATION MASTER: Here she comes!
>
> (Long shot) Engine appearing round bend.
>
> EXTERIOR. STATION. DAY
> Johnny tethers his horse.
>
> ANNIE-BELLE: Why, Johnny, you've come to
> say goodbye after all!
>
> (Close up) Johnny, racked with emotion.
>
> JOHNNY: He shan't have you. He'll never
> have you. Here's where you belong, with
> me. Out here.

Giovanni: Thus die, and die by me, and by my hand!
  Revenge is mine; honour doth love command!
Annabella: Oh, brother, by your hand!

> EXTERIOR. STATION. DAY
> ANNIE-BELLE: Don't shoot – think of the
> baby! Don't –

MINISTER'S SON: Oh, my God –

Bang, bang, bang.

Thinking to protect his wife, the young husband threw his arms around her and so he died, by a split second, before the second bullet pierced her and both fell to the ground as the engine wheezed to a halt and passengers came tumbling off to see what Wild West antics were being played out while the parents stood and stared and did not believe, did not believe.

Seeing some life left in his sister, Johnny sank to his knees beside her and her eyes opened up and, perhaps, she saw him, for she said:

Annabella: Brother, unkind, unkind . . .

So that Death would be well satisfied, Johnny then put the barrel of the rifle into his mouth and pulled the trigger.

EXTERIOR. STATION. DAY
(Crane shot) The three bodies, the Minister comforting his wife, the passengers crowding off the train in order to look at the catastrophe.

The 'Love Theme' rises over a pan of the prairie under the vast sky, the green breast of the continent, the earth, beloved, cruel, unkind.

NOTE:

The Old World John Ford made Giovanni cut out Annabella's heart and carry it on stage; the stage direction reads: *Enter Giovanni, with a heart upon his dagger.* The New World John Ford would have no means of representing this scene on celluloid, although it is irresistibly reminiscent of the ritual tortures practised by the Indians who lived here before.

Gun for the Devil

A hot, dusty, flyblown Mexican border town – a town without hope, without grace, the end of the road for all those who've the misfortune to find themselves washed up here. The time is about the turn of the century, long after the heroic period of the West is past; and there was never anything heroic about these border raiders, this poverty-stricken half-life they lead. The Mendozas, a barbarous hierarchy of bandits, run the town, its corrupt sheriff, its bank, the telegraph – everything. Even the priest is an appointment of theirs.

The only establishment in the town with a superficial veneer of elegance is the bar-cum-whorehouse. This is presided over by a curious, apparently ill-matched couple – an ageing, drunken, consumptive European aristocrat and his mistress, the madame, who keeps him. She's called Roxana, a straightforward, ageing, rather raddled, unimaginative, affectionate woman.

She is the sister of Maria Mendoza, the bandit's wife – that's how she obtained the brothel concession. Roxana and her man, the dying, despairing man they call the Count, arrived, the pair of them, out of nowhere, a few years back, penniless, in rags; they'd begged a ride in a farm cart . . . 'I've come home, Maria, after all this time . . . there's nowhere else to go.' Roxana'd had a lot of experience in the trade; with her brother-in-law's blessing, with his finance, she opened up a bar-cum-brothel and staffed it with girls who'd got good reason to lie low for a while – not, perhaps, the best class of whore. Five of them. But they suit the customers very well; they keep Mendoza's desperadoes out of trouble, they service his visitors – and sometimes there's a casual visitor, a stray passerby, a travelling salesman, say, or a smuggler. The brothel prospers.

And the Count, in his soiled, ruffled shirts and threadbare suits of dandified black, lends a little class to the joint; so his life has come to this, he serves to ornament his mistress's bar. A certain bitterness, a dour dignity, characterises the Count.

The Count lets visitors buy drinks for him; he is a soak, but a distinguished one, nevertheless. He keeps a margin of distance about himself – he has his pride, still, even if he's dying. He's rumoured to have been, in his day, in the Old Country, a legendary marksman. The girls chatter among themselves. Julie, the Yankee, says she's heard that he and Roxana used to do an act in a circus. He used to shoot all her clothes off her until she was as naked as the day she was born. As the day she was born!

But hadn't he killed Roxana's lover, no, not her lover but some man she'd been sold to, some seamy story . . . wasn't it in San Francisco, on the waterfront? No, no, no – everything happened in Austria, or Germany, or wherever it is he comes from, long before he met Roxana. He's not touched a gun since he met Roxana. He never shoots, now, even if his old-fashioned, long-barrelled rifle hangs on the wall . . . look! He was *too good* a shot; they said that only the devil himself – it's best not to pay attention to such stories, even if Maddalena once worked in a house in San Francisco where Roxana used to work and somebody told her – but the Count's shadow falls across the wall; they hush, even if Maddalena furtively crosses herself.

In this town, nobody asks any questions. Who would live here if they had the option to live anywhere else? Poor

Teresa Mendoza, pretty as a picture, sweet sixteen, sullen, dissatisfied, she got a few ideas above her station when they sent her off to a convent to learn how to read and write. What does she need to read and write for? Not when she's condemned to live like a pig. But she's going to get married, isn't she? To a rich man? Yes, but he's a rich bandit!

In the afternoon, the slack time, Roxana and her sister sit in Roxana's boudoir with the shades down against the glaring sun, rocking on cane rocking-chairs, smoking cigars together and gently tippling tequila. Maria Mendoza is a roaring, mannish, booted and spurred bandit herself; savage, illiterate, mother of one daughter only, the beautiful Teresa. 'We finally fixed it, Maria; signed, sealed and almost delivered ... See, here's the picture of Teresa's fiancé ... isn't he a handsome man? Eh? Eh?'

Roxana looks at the cherished photograph dubiously. Another bandit, even if a more powerful one than Mendoza himself! At least she, Roxana, has managed to get herself a man who doesn't wear spurs to bed. And Teresa hasn't even met her intended ... 'No, no!' cries Maria. 'That's not necessary. Love will come, as soon as they're married, once he gets his leg over her ... and the babies, my Teresa's babies, my grandchildren, growing up in his enormous house, surrounded by servants bowing and scraping.' But Roxana is less certain and shakes her head doubtfully. 'Anyway, there's nothing Teresa can do about it,' says her mother firmly; 'it's all been fixed up by Mendoza, she'll be the bandit queen of the entire border. That's a lot better than living like a pig in this hole.'

The Mendozas do indeed live like pigs, behind a stockade, in a filthy, gipsy-like encampment of followers and hangers-on in the grounds of what was once, before the Mendozas took it over, a rather magnificent Spanish colonial hacienda. Now Mendoza himself, Teresa's hulking brute of a father, gallops his horse down the corridors, shoots out the windowpanes in his drunkenness. Teresa, the spoiled only daughter, screams at him in fury: 'We live like pigs! Like pigs!'

Problems in the brothel! The pianist has run off with the prettiest of all the girls; they're heading south to start up their own place, she reckons her husband won't chase her down as far as Acapulco. They wait for the stagecoach to take them away, sitting on barrels in the general store with their bags piled around them; the coach drops one passenger, the driver goes off to water the horses. Any work here for a piano player? Why, what a coincidence!

He's from the north, a gringo. And a city boy, too, in a velvet coat, with such long, white fingers! He winces when he hears gunfire – a Mendoza employee boisterously shooting at chickens in the gutter. How pale he is . . . a handsome boy, nice, refined, educated voice. Is there even the trace of a foreign accent?

Like the Count, he is startlingly alien in this primitive, semi-desert environment.

Roxana melts maternally at the sight of him; he delights the Count by playing a little Brahms on the out-of-tune, honky-tonk piano. The Count's eyes mist over; he remembers . . . The conservatoire at Vienna? Can it be possible? How extraordinary . . . so you were studying at the conservatoire at Vienna? Although Roxana's delighted with her new employee, her lip curls, she is a natural sceptic. But he's the best piano-player she's ever heard.

And, anyway, nobody really asks questions in this town, or believes any answers, for that matter. He must have his reasons for holing up in this godforsaken place. The job's yours, Johnny; you get a little room over the porch to sleep in, with a lock on it to keep the girls out. They get bored . . . don't let them bother you.

But Johnny is in the grip of a singular passion; he is a grim and dedicated being. He ignores the girls completely.

In his bedroom, Johnny places photographs of a man and a woman – his parents – on the splintered pine dressing-table; pins up a poster for the San Francisco Opera House on the wall, *Der Freischütz*. He addresses the photographs. 'I've found out where they live, I've tracked them to their lair. It won't be long now, Mother and Father. Not long.'

Hoofbeats outside. Maria Mendoza is coming to visit her sister, riding astride, like a man, while her daughter rides side-saddle like a lady, even if her hair is an uncombed haystack. She looks the wild bandit-child she is. But – now she's an engaged woman, her father forbids her to visit the brothel, even to pay a formal call on her good aunt! Ride back home, Teresa!

Sullen, she turns her horse round. Looking back at the brothel as she trots away, she sees Johnny gazing at her from his window; their eyes meet, Johnny's briefly veil.

Teresa is momentarily confused; then spurs her horse cruelly, gallops off, like a wild thing.

In the small hours, when the brothel has finally closed down for the night, Johnny plays Chopin for the Count. Tears of sentimental nostalgia roll down the old man's cheeks. And Vienna ... is it still the same? Try not to remember ... he pours himself another whisky. Then Johnny asks him softly, is it true what he's heard ... stories circulating in the faraway Austro-Hungarian Empire; the Count starts.

The old legend, about the man who makes a pact with the devil to obtain a bullet that cannot miss its target ...

An old legend, says the Count. In the superstitious villages, they believe such things still.

All kinds of shadows drift in through the open window.

The old legend, given a new lease of life by the exploits of a certain aristocrat, who vanished suddenly, left everything. And the Mendozas, here, the bandits — aren't they all damned? Vicious, cruel . . . wouldn't a man who's sold his soul to the devil feel safest amongst the damned? Amongst whores and murderers?

The Count, shuddering, pours yet another whisky.

Is it true what they used to whisper, that the Count — this Count, you! old man — had a reputation as a marksman so extraordinary that everyone thought he had supernatural powers?

The Count, recovering himself, says: 'They said that of Paganini, that he must have learned how to play the fiddle from the devil. Since no human being could have played so well.'

'And perhaps he did,' says Johnny.

'You're a musician, not a murderer, Johnny.'

'Stranglers and piano-players both need long fingers. But a bullet is more merciful,' suggests Johnny obliquely.

Out of some kind of dream into which he's abruptly sunk, the Count says: 'The seventh bullet belongs to the devil. That is how you pay —'

But tonight, he won't, can't say any more. He lurches off to bed, to Roxana, who's waiting for him, as she always does. But why, oh why, is the old man crying? The whisky makes you into a baby . . . but Roxana takes care of you, she's always taken care of you, ever since she found you.

Roxana mothers the newcomer, Johnny, too, but she also watches him, with troubled eyes. All he does is play the piano and brood obsessively over the Mendoza gunmen as they sport and play in the bar. Sometimes he inspects the Count's old rifle, hung up on the wall, strokes the barrel, caresses the stock; but he knows nothing about the arts of death at all. Nothing! And he takes no interest in the girls, that's unhealthy.

It seems to Roxana that there's a likeness between her old man and the young one. That crazy, black-clad dignity. They always seem to be chatting to one another and sometimes they talk in German. Roxana hates that, it makes her feel shut out, excluded.

Can he be, can young Johnny be . . . some son the Count begot and then abandoned, a child he'd never known, come all this way to find him?

Could it be?

Old man and young one, with eyes the same shape, hands the same shape . . . could it be?

And if it is, why don't they tell her, Roxana?

Secrets make her feel shut out, excluded. She sits in her room on the rocking-chair in the dusk, sipping tequila.

Voices below – in German. She goes to her window, watches the Count and the piano-player wander off together in the direction of the little scummy pond in front of the brothel, which is set back off the main street.

She crosses herself, goes on rocking.

'Speak English, we must leave the Old World and its mysteries behind us,' says the Count. 'The old, weary, exhausted world. Leave it behind! This is a new country, full of hope . . .'

He is heavily ironic. The ancient rocks of the desert lour down in the sunset.

'But the landscape of this country is more ancient by far than we are, strange gods brood over it. I shall never be friends with it, never.'

Aliens, strangers, the Count and Johnny watch the Mendozas ride out on the rampage, led by Teresa's father; a band of grizzled hooligans, firing off their guns, shouting.

Johnny, calm, quiet, tells the Count how the Mendozas

killed his parents when they raided a train for the gold the train carried. His parents, both opera singers, on their way back across the continent from California, from a booking in San Francisco . . . and he far away, in Europe.

Mendoza himself tore the earrings from his mother's ears. And raped her. And somebody shot his father when his father tried to stop the rape. And then they shot his mother because she was screaming so loudly.

Calm, quiet, Johnny recounts all.

'We all have our tragedies.'

'Some tragedies we can turn back on the perpetrators. I've planned my revenge. A suitably operatic revenge. I shall seduce the beautiful señorita and give her a baby. And if I can't shoot her father and mother, I shall find some way of strangling them with my beautiful pianist's hands.'

Quiet, assured, deadly – but incompetent. He doesn't know one end of a gun from the other; never raised his hand in anger in his life.

But he's been brooding on this revenge ever since the black-edged letter arrived at his lodgings in Vienna; in Vienna, where he heard how a nobleman made a pact with the devil, once, to ensure no bullet he ever fired would miss the mark . . .

'If you've planned it all so well, if you're dedicated to your vengeance . . .'

Johnny nods. Quiet, assured, deadly.

'If you're quite determined, then . . . you belong to the devil already. And a bullet is indeed more merciful than anger, if accurately fired.'

And the Count has always hated Mendoza's contempt for himself and Roxana, who live on Mendoza's charity.

But Johnny has never used a gun in his life. Old man, old man, what have you to lose? You've nothing, you've come to a dead end, kept by a whore in a flyblown town at the end of all the roads you ever took . . . give me a gun that will never miss a shot; that will fire by itself. I know you know how to get one. I know –

'I have nothing to lose,' says the Count inscrutably. 'Except my sins, Johnny. Except my sins.'

Teresa, sixteen, sullen, pretty, dissatisfied, retreats into her bedroom, into the depths of an enormous, gilded, four-poster bed looted from a train especially for her, surrounded by a jackdaw's nest of tawdry, looted glitter, gorges herself on chocolates, leafs through very very old fashion magazines. She hugs a scrawny kitten, her pet. Chickens roost on the canopy of her bed. Maa! maa! a goat pokes its head in through the open window. Teresa twitches with annoyance. You call this living?

Her door bursts open. An excited dog follows a flock of squawking chickens into the room; all the chickens roosting on the bed rise up, squawking. Chaos! The dog jumps on to the bed, begins to gnaw at the bloody something he carries in his mouth. Kitten rises on its hind legs to bat at the dog. Teresa hurls chocolates, magazines, screaming – insupportable! She storms out of the room.

In the courtyard, her mother is slaughtering a screaming pig. That's the sort of thing the Mendoza womenfolk enjoy! Ugh. Teresa's made for better things, she knows it.

She wanders disconsolately out into the dusty street. Empty. Like my life, like my life.

Willows bend over the scummy pool in front of Roxana's brothel; it has a secluded air.

Teresa skulks beside the pool, sullenly throwing stones at her own reflection. Morning, slack time; in voluptuous deshabille, the whores lean over the veranda: 'Little Teresa! Little Teresa! Come in and see your auntie!' They laugh at her in her black stockings, her convent-girl dress, her rumpled hair.

Roxana's doing the books, behind the bar, with a pair of wire-rimmed glasses propped on her nose. The Count pours himself elevenses – she looks up, is about to remonstrate with him, thinks better of it, returns to her sums. Morning sunshine; outside on the veranda, the whores giggle and wave at Teresa.

Johnny idly begins to play a Strauss waltz. Roxana's foot taps a little.

The Count puts down his whisky. Smiles. He approaches Roxana, presents his arm. She's startled – then blushes, beams like a young girl. Takes off her glasses, pats her hair, glances at herself in the mirror behind the bar, pleasantly flustered. Seeing her pleasure, the Count becomes more courtly still. Still quite a fine figure of a man! And she, when she smiles, you see what a pretty girl she must have been.

Johnny flourishes the keys; he's touched. He begins to play a Strauss waltz in earnest.

Roxana takes the Count's proffered arm; they dance.

'Look! Look! Roxana's dancing!'

The whores flock back into the room, laughing, admiring. And begin to dance with one another, girl with girl, in their soiled negligées, their unlaced corsets, petticoats, torn stockings.

Maddalena, partnerless, lingers on the veranda, teasing Teresa. Music spills out of the brothel.

'Teresa! Teresa! Come and dance with me!'

Slowly, slowly, Teresa arrives at the veranda, climbs the stairs, peers through a window as, flushed and breathless, the dancers collapse in a laughing heap.

She and Johnny exchange a flashing glance. But her aunt

catches sight of her. 'Teresa, Teresa, scram! This is no place for you!'

At the Mendozas' dinner-table, her father sits picking his teeth with his knife.

'I want to learn the piano, papa.'

He continues to pick his teeth with his knife. She didn't want to learn the piano at the damn convent; why does she want to learn it now? To be a lady, Papa; isn't she going to have a grand wedding, marry a fine man? 'Papa, I want to learn the piano.'

Teresa is spoiled, indulged in everything. But her father likes to tease her; he'll drag out her pleading as long as he can. He doesn't often have his daughter pleading with him. He cuts himself a chunk more meat, munches.

'And who will teach you piano in this hole, hm?'

'Johnny. Johnny at Aunt Roxana's.'

He's suddenly really angry. You see what an animal he can become.

'What? My daughter learn piano in a brothel? Under the eye of that fat whore, Roxana?'

Maria leaps to her sister's defence, surging down on her husband with the carving knife held high. 'Don't you insult my sister!'

Mendoza twists her wrist; she drops the knife. 'I'm not having my daughter mixing with whores!'

'I want to learn piano,' the spoiled child insists.

'Over my dead body will you go to Roxana's to learn the piano, not now you are an engaged girl.'

'Then, papa, buy me a piano, let Johnny come here to teach me.'

A creaking wagon delivers a shiny, new, baby grand in the courtyard of the rotting hacienda, among the grunting pigs and flapping chickens.

Effortfully, it's installed in Teresa's room; entranced, she picks at the notes. 'Kitty, kitty, the young man in the black jacket is coming to teach me piano . . .'

Her mother chaperones her, sitting, lolling in a rocking chair, sipping tequila. Johnny, neat, elegant, a stranger, damned, with a portfolio of music under his arm, has come to give Teresa lessons. First, scales . . . soon, Czerny exercises. Johnny waits, watchful, biding his time.

Bored, her mother sips tequila and nods off to sleep . . . A Czerny exercise; Teresa hasn't quite mastered it. Making a mess of it, in fact. On purpose? Johnny's presence makes her flutter.

Johnny stands behind her, showing her where to put her hands. His long, white hands cover her little, brown paws with the bitten fingernails.

She turns to him. They kiss. She's eager, willing; he's surprised by her enthusiasm, almost taken aback. Despises her. It's going to be almost too easy!

But where is the seduction to be accomplished? Not in Teresa's bedroom, with her mother dozing in the armchair. Not in Johnny's room at the brothel, either, under Aunt Roxana's watchful eye.

'In church, Johnny; nobody will look for lovers there.'

A huge, cavernous, almost cathedral, built in expectation of mass conversions among the Indians, now almost in ruins, on a kind of bluff, brooding over the half-ruined village. Empty. And they make love on the floor of the church, the savage child, the vengeance-seeker. Afterwards, triumphant, she buries her face in his breast, shrieking for glee; he is detached, rejoicing in his own coldness, his own wickedness.

Naked, Teresa wanders down the aisle of the church towards the altar, stands looking up vaguely at the rococo Christ. She pokes out her tongue at her saviour.

'I'll be here again, soon. I'm going to be married.'

'Married?'

'To a fine bandit gentleman.' Makes a face. 'Because I have no brothers, I am the heiress. My son will inherit everything, but first I must be married.'

'Oh, no,' says Johnny, lost, gone into his vengeance. 'You won't be married. I won't let you be married.'

Suspicious, at first. Then . . . 'Do you love me?' Exultant, shouting. 'So you love me! You must love me! You'll take me away!'

The Count rummages through a trunk in his and Roxana's bedroom, he gets out old books and curious instruments. The room is full of mysterious shadows. Roxana tries the door, finds that it is locked; she rattles the handle agitatedly. 'What are you up to ? What secrets do you have from me? Is it the old secret? Is it –'

The Count lets her in, takes her into his arms. 'He'll take the burden from me, Roxana. He wants to, he's willing, he knows . . .'

'Your . . . son has come to set you free?'

'Not my son, Roxana.'

She is so relieved that she almost forgets the dark import of what he's saying. Yet she must ask him: 'And what's the price?'

'High, Roxana. Do you love a poor old man, do you love him more than you love your kin?'

Wide-eyed, she stares at him.

'Yes, old man, I do believe I do. It's been so long, now, since we've been together . . .'

'We'll be together for ever, Roxana.'

So he goes on assembling his occult materials and now she helps him. She has only one reservation. 'The little Teresa, nothing must happen to her . . .'

'No. Not Teresa. What harm has she ever done to anyone? Not Teresa.'

An eclipse of the moon. In the church, in darkness, at the altar, the Count and Johnny summon the appropriate demon – the Archer of the Dark Abyss. Such a storm! Out of nowhere, a great wind, whirling the dust into a sandstorm. Roxana, alone in her bedroom full of curious shadows, draws the shutters close and mutters prayers, incantations.

The great wind blows open the doors of the church, sets them creaking on their hinges. Out of the sandstorm, hallucinatory figures emerge and merge, figures of demons or gods not necessarily those of Europe. The unknown continent, the new world, issues forth its banned daemonology.

The Count has summoned up more than he bargained for. He and Johnny crouch in the pentacle; Aztec and Toltec gods appear in giant forms. The church seems to have disappeared.

When the ritual is done, all clears; the interior of the church is a shambles, however, the Christ over the altar cast down on its face. Johnny and the Count pick themselves up from the floor, where the wind has left them. The Count is coughing horribly, his face is livid; the rite has nearly killed him.

Outside, all is calm now, a clear, bright night. The moon is back in the heavens again. Johnny, a man in the grip of a mania, stern, firm, helps the shaking Count to his feet.

'Where is the weapon?'

'He has come. He's waiting. He'll give it to us.'

Outside, against the wall, so still he's almost part of the landscape, an Indian sits in the dark, poncho, slouch hat, waiting, impassive.

The Count, leaning heavily on Johnny, greets the Indian

with some courtly ceremony. But Johnny barks: 'Got the gun?'

'I got it.'

The gun changes hands. Johnny grabs it.

'How much?'

'On account,' says the Indian and grins. 'On account.'

He tips his hat. His pony, in the graveyard, grazes on a grave. The two Europeans watch him walk towards his pony, mount, ride. In the immense stillness of the night, his hoofbeats diminish.

Johnny inspects the Winchester repeater in his hands; it looks perfectly normal. Not used to guns, he handles it clumsily. His disappointment is obvious.

'What's so special about it? Could have bought one in the store.'

'It will fire seven bullets,' says the Count, impassive as any Indian. 'And the seventh bullet is the one that *he* put in it, it belongs to him.'

'But –'

'The seventh bullet is the devil's own. He will fire the seventh shot for you, even though you pull the trigger. But the other six can't miss their targets. Though you've never used a gun before.'

Incredulous, Johnny takes aim, fires at a movement in the darkness. He rushes towards the scream. His target, Teresa's kitten, dead.

'Five left now, for your own use,' says the Count. 'Use them sparingly. They come at a high price.'

Teresa wants her kitten. 'Kitty! Kitty!' But the kitten doesn't come. 'The dogs have eaten it,' says Teresa's mother. 'And hold still, Teresa, you're wriggling like an eel; how can I fit your wedding-dress . . .?'

It's a store-bought wedding dress, come on the stage-coach from Mexico City. All white lace. And a veil! In front of the clouded mirror in Teresa's bedroom, Maria pops the veil on her daughter's head; what a picture. But Teresa sulks.

'I don't want to get married.'

Too bad, Teresa! Tomorrow you must and will get married.

I won't. I won't!

You won't wheedle your father out of this one, not this time.

Teresa, in her wedding finery, picks out a few notes of the 'Wedding March' on her piano; furious, she slams the lid shut.

Johnny, at the piano in the whorehouse, plays a few bars of the 'Wedding March'; a wedding guest, drunk, flings his glass at the mirror behind the bar, smashing it. The whores superstitiously huddle and mutter. The place is packed out with wedding guests, all notable villains. But there is too much tension to be any joy. Roxana, unsmiling, rings up the price of a replacement mirror on her cash register. The Count, morose, stoops over his drink at the bar. The wedding guests treat him with genial contempt.

Teresa creeps out of her bedroom window, steals along the street, conceals herself hastily in the shadows where an Indian on a pony comes riding down the street.

Her lover waits for her by the scummy pond. Take me away. Save me! He strokes her hair with the first sign of tenderness. Perhaps he *will* take her away, if she can bear to look at him after the holocaust. Perhaps . . .

It's very late, now. Only the Count stays up. He's gazing at the recumbent form of a wedding guest passed out on the floor, snoring. The whores have stuck a feather hat on

the visitor's head, taken off his trousers, daubed his face
with rouge.

When Johnny comes in, the Count silently pours him a
drink. He looks at the boy with, almost, love – certainly
with some emotion.

'I could almost ask you . . .'

Johnny smiles, shakes his head, whistles a few bars of
Chopin's 'Funeral March'.

'But then . . . be good to the little Teresa. "The prince of
darkness is a gentleman . . ." '

Maybe. Maybe not. But, maybe . . .

How Teresa's hair tangles in the comb! A great bustle in
the Mendoza encampment; they've got a carriage for her,
decked it with exuberant paper flowers. But she herself is
nervous, anxious; she chews at her underlip, she lets the
women dress her as if she were a doll. Her mother, oddly
respectable in black, weeps copiously. Teresa, in her wedding dress and veil, suddenly turns to her mother and hugs
her convulsively. The woman returns the embrace fiercely.

Johnny kisses the photographs of his father and mother.
It's time. Unhandily carrying the rifle, in his music-student's
black velvet jacket, elegant, deadly, mad, he goes towards
the church.

They've put back the rococo, suffering Christ; Johnny
crouches beneath him, hiding under the skirts of the altar
cloth. He tests the weight of the gun in his hand, peers
through the sights.

The Count won't go to the wedding. No, he won't! He
won't get out of bed. Please, Roxana, don't you go to the
wedding, either! What? Not see my little niece Teresa get

married? And you should come, too, you irreligious old man. Aren't you fond of Teresa?

But the Count is sick this morning. He can't crawl out of bed. He coughs, stares at the ominous bloodstains on his handkerchief.

'I'm dying, Roxana. Don't leave me.'

Though the bridegroom has arrived already, a huge brute, the image of Teresa's father. He takes his place before the altar. The congregation rustles. The organ plays softly.

Roxana, late, troubled, untidily dressed, slips in at the back of the church.

Teresa steps out of the flower-decorated carriage in front of the church. She's really worried, now, looking desperately around for Johnny. Her mother kisses her, again; this time, the girl doesn't respond, she's got too much on her mind. Her mother and the Mendoza womenfolk enter the church. Her father, a little dressed up, boots polished, offers her his arm.

Traditional gasps as she walks down the aisle – isn't she lovely! Even if her eyes search round and round the church for her rescuer. Where can he be? What will he do to save me?

The organ rings out.

Teresa arrives beside her bridegroom. From beneath her veil, she gives him a swift glance of furious dislike. The priest says the first words of the wedding service.

Johnny flings back the altar cloth, leaps on to the altar, shoots point-blank the wide-eyed, open-mouthed Mendoza.

Mendoza tumbles backwards down the altar steps.

Silence. Then, shouting. Then, gunfire. Havoc!

But no bullet can touch Johnny; he shoots the bridegroom as the bridegroom leaps forward to attack him;

shoots three – four – into the crowd of Mendoza desperadoes, two men fall.

Teresa, in her wedding finery, stands speechless, shocked.

Her mother, wailing, rushes from the crowd towards her
dead husband.

Johnny aims, shoots Maria. She drops dead on to the
body of her husband.

Teresa at last wakes up. She rushes through the havoc in
the church; she is appalled, the world has come to an end.

Roxana fights free of the crowd and goes running after
her. The church is a mêlée of shots, noise, gunsmoke.

Outside the church, the girl and woman meet. Teresa
can't speak. Roxana hugs her, grabs her hand, pulls her
down the path, towards the whorehouse.

Johnny erupts from the church door. Now he's like a
mad dog. Blazing, furious, deadly – carrying a gun.

By the scummy pool, Roxana hears Johnny coming after
them. She drags Teresa faster, faster – the girl stumbles
over her white lace hem, now filthy with dust and blood.
Faster, faster – he's coming, the murderer's coming, the
devil himself is coming!

The Count's mistress and the beloved little Teresa run
towards the whorehouse, where the Count gazes out of the
window; run towards him, with the madman hot on their
heels.

The Count opens the whorehouse door.

He's carrying the rifle that hangs on the wall of the bar.

Slowly, shakily, he raises it.

He's aiming at Johnny.

Teresa sees him, breaks free of Roxana's hand, dashes
back towards her lover – to try to protect him? Some
reason, sufficient to her hysteria.

Johnny, startled, halts; so the old man's turned against

him, has he? The old man's turned his own magic rifle on the young one, the acolyte!

He takes aim at the Count, fires the seventh bullet.

He's forgotten it's the seventh bullet, forgotten everything except the sudden ease with which he can kill.

He fires the seventh bullet and Teresa drops dead by the side of the scummy pool. Her lace train slides down into the water.

The Count bursts into a great fit of tears. Roxana kneels by the dead girl, uselessly speaks to her, closes her eyes gently. Crosses herself. Gives the weeping Count, slumped on the whorehouse veranda, a long, dark look.

The crowd spills out of the church.

Johnny drops his gun, turns, runs.

Coda

Almost the desert. White, fantastic rocks, sand, burning sun. Johnny stole one of the Mendozas' horses; now it founders beneath him. He shades his eyes; there's a village in the distance . . .

But this village seems deserted. A weird, shabby figure in his music-student's black jacket, he draws water from the well, drinks. At last, a thin, ragged, filthy child emerges from a derelict house.

'The smallpox came. All dead, all dead.'

Flies buzz on an unburied corpse in a murky interior. Johnny retches. He's white-faced, fevered – you would have said, a man with the devil pursuing him.

At the end of the village, gazing across the acres of desert before him, a figure is propped against the wall, a figure so still, so silent as at first to seem part of the landscape. He smiles to see Johnny stumbling towards him.

'I was waiting for you,' says the Indian who sold Johnny the gun. 'We have some business to conclude.'

The Merchant of Shadows

I killed the car. And at once provoked such sudden, resonant quiet as if, when I switched off the ignition, I myself brought into being the shimmering late afternoon hush, the ripening sun, the very Pacific that, way below, at the foot of the cliff, shattered its foamy peripheries with the sound of a thousand distant cinema organs.

I'd never get used to California. After three years, still the enchanted visitor. However frequently I had been disappointed, I still couldn't help it, I still tingled with expectation, still always thought that something wonderful might happen.

Call me the Innocent Abroad.

All the same, you can take the boy out of London but you can't take London out of the boy. You will find my grasp of the local lingo enthusiastic but shaky. I call gas 'petrol', and so on. I don't intend to go native, I'm not here for good, I'm here upon a pilgrimage. I have hied me, like a holy palmer, from the dishevelled capital of a foggy, three-cornered island on the other side of the world where the light is only good for water-colourists to this place where, to wax metaphysical about it, Light was made Flesh.

I am a student of Light and Illusion. That is, of cinema. When first I clapped my eyes on that HOLLYWOODLAND sign back in the city now five hours' hard drive distant, I thought I'd glimpsed the Holy Grail.

And now, as if it were the most everyday thing in the

world, I was on my way to meet a legend. A living legend, who roosted on this lonely clifftop like a forlorn seabird.

I was parked in a gravelled lot where the rough track I'd painfully negotiated since I left the minor road that brought me from the freeway terminated. I shared the parking lot with a small, red, crap-caked Toyota truck that, some time ago, had seen better days. There was straw in the back. Funny kind of transportation for a legend. But I knew she was in there, behind the gated wall in front of me, and I needed a little time alone with the ocean before the tryst began. I climbed out of the car and crept close to the edge of the precipice.

The ocean shushed and tittered like an audience when the lights dim before the main feature.

The first time I saw the Pacific, I'd had a vision of sea gods, but not the ones *I* knew, oh, no. Not even Botticelli's prime 36B cup blonde ever came in on *this* surf. My entire European mythology capsized under the crash of waves Britannia never ruled and then I knew that the denizens of these deeps are *sui generis* and belong to no mythology but their weird own. They have the strangest eyes, lenses on stalks that go flicker, flicker, and give you the truth twenty-four times a second. Their torsos luminesce in every shade of technicolor but have no depth, no substance, no dimensionality. Beings from a wholly strange pantheon. Beautiful – but alien.

Aliens were somewhat on my mind, however, perhaps because I was somewhat alienated myself in LA, but also due to the obsession of my room-mate. While I researched my thesis, I was rooming back there in the city in an apartment over a New Age bookshop-cum-healthfood restaurant with a science fiction freak I'd met at a much earlier stage of studenthood during the chance intimacy of the mutual runs in Barcelona. Now he and I subsisted on brown rice courtesy of the Japanese waitress from downstairs, with whom we were both on, ahem, intimate terms, and he was always talking about aliens. He thought most of the people you met on the streets were aliens cunningly simulating human beings. He thought the Venusians were behind it.

He said he had tested Hiroko's reality quotient sufficiently and *she* was clear, but I guessed from his look he wasn't too sure about me. That shared diarrhoea in the Plaza Real was proving a shaky bond. I stayed out of the place as much as possible. I kept my head down at school all day and tried to manifest humanity as well as I knew how whenever I came home for a snack, a shower and, if I got the chance, one of Hiroko's courteous if curiously impersonal embraces. Now my host showed signs of getting into leather. Would it soon be time to move?

It must be the light that sends them crazy, that white light now refracting from the sibilant Pacific, the precious light that, when it is distilled, becomes the movies. *Ars Magna Lucis et Umbrae*, the Great Art of Light and Shade as Athanias Kircher put it, he who tinkered with magic lanterns four centuries ago in the Gothic north.

And from that Gothic north had come the object of the quest that brought me to this luminous hill-top – a long-dead Teutonic illusionist who'd played with light and shade as well as any. You know him as Hank Mann, that 'dark genius of the screen', the director with 'the occult touch', that neglected giant etc. etc. etc.

But stay, you may ask, how can a dead man, no matter how occult his touch, be the object of a quest?

Aha! In that cliff-top house he'd left the woman, part of whose legend was she was his widow.

He had been her ultimate husband. First (silent movies) she'd hitched up with an acrobatic cowboy and, when a pinto threw him, she'd joined a *soi-disant* Viennese tenor for a season of kitschissimo musicals during early sound. Hank Mann turned her into an icon after he rescued her off a cardboard crag where he'd come upon her, yodelling. When Mann passed on, she shut up marital shop entirely, and her screen presence acquired the frozen majesty of one appreciating, if somewhat belatedly, the joys of abstinence. She never did another on-screen love scene, either.

If you are a true buff, you know that he was born Heinrich Mannheim. One or two titles in two or three catalogues survive from his early days at UFA, plus a handful of scratched, faded stills.

My correspondence with his relict, conducted through somebody who p.p.d for her in an illegible scrawl, finally produced this invitation. I'd been half-stunned with joy. I was, you understand, writing my thesis about Mannheim. He had become my pet, my hobby, my obsession.

But you must understand that I was prevaricating out of pure nerves. For she was far, far more than a Hollywood widow; she was the Star of Stars, no less, the greatest of them all . . . dubbed by *Time* magazine the 'Spirit of the Cinema' when, on her eightieth birthday, she graced its cover for the seventh time, with a smile like open day in a porcelain factory and a white lace mantilla on the curls that time had bleached with its inexorable peroxide. And had she not invited little me, me! to call for a chat, a drink, at this ambiguous hour, martini-time, the blue hour, when you fold up the day and put it away and shake out the exciting night?

Only surely she was well past the expectation of exciting times. She had become what Hiroko's people call a 'living national treasure'. Decade after ageless decade, movie after movie, 'the greatest star in heaven'. That was the promo. She'd no especial magic, either. She was no Gish, nor Brooks, nor Dietrich, nor Garbo, who all share the same gift, the ability to reveal otherness. She *did* have a certain touch-me-not thing, that made her a natural for *film noir* in the Forties. Otherwise, she possessed only the extraordinary durability of her presence, as if continually incarnated afresh with the passage of time due to some occult operation of the Great Art of Light and Shade.

One odd thing. As Svengali, Hank Mann had achieved a posthumous success. Although it was he who had brushed her with stardust (she'd been a mere 'leading player' up till then), her career only acquired that touch of the fabulous after he adjourned to the great cutting room in the sky.

There was a scent of jasmine blowing over the wall from an invisible garden. I deeply ingested breath. I checked out my briefcase: notebook, recorder, tapes. I checked that the recorder contained tape. I was nervous as hell. And then there was nothing for it but, briefcase in hand, to summon the guts to stride up to her gate.

It was an iron gate with a sheet of zinc behind the wrought squiggles so you couldn't see through and, when I reached up to ring the bell, this gate creaked open of its own accord to let me in and then swung to behind me with a disconcerting, definitive clang. So there I was.

A plane broke the darkening dish of sky, that sealed up again behind it. Inside the garden, it was very quiet. Nobody came to meet me.

A flight of rough-cut stone steps led up to a pool surrounded by clumps of sweet-smelling weeds; I recognised lavender. A tree or two dropped late summer leaves on scummy water and, when I saw that pool, I couldn't help it, I started to shiver; I'll tell you why in a minute. That untended pool, in which a pair of dark glasses with one cracked lens rested on an emerald carpet of algae, along with an empty gin bottle.

On the terrace, a couple of rusty, white-enamelled chairs,

a lop-sided table. Then, fringed by a clump of cryptomeria, the house von Mannheim caused to be erected for his bride.

That house made the Bauhaus look baroque. An austere cube of pure glass, it exhibited the geometry of transparency at its most severe. Yet, just at that moment, it took all the red light of the setting sun into itself and flashed like a ruby slipper. I knew the wall of the vast glittering lounge gaped open to admit me, and only me, but I thought, well, if nobody has any objections, I'll just stick around on the terrace for a while, keep well away from that glass box that looks like nothing so much as the coffin for a classical modernist Snow White; let the lady come out to me.

No sound but the deep, distant bass of the sea; a gull or two; pines, hushing one another.

So I waited. And waited. And I found myself wondering just what it was the scent of jasmine reminded me of, in order to take my mind off what I knew damn well the swimming pool reminded me of – *Sunset Boulevard*, of course. And I knew damn well, of course I knew, that this was indeed the very pool in which my man Hank Mann succumbed back in 1940, so very long ago, when not even I nor my blessed mother, yet, was around to so much as piss upon the floor.

I waited until I found myself growing impatient. How does one invoke the Spirit of Cinema? Burn a little offering of popcorn and old fan magazines? Offer a libation of Jeyes' Fluid mixed with Kia Ora orange?

I found myself vengefully asserting that I knew one or two things about her old man that perhaps she never knew herself. For example, his grandmother's maiden name (Ernst). I knew he entered UFA and swept the cutting-room floor. I talked to the son he left behind in Germany shortly after conceiving him. Nice old buffer, early sixties, retired bank clerk, prisoner of war in Norfolk, England, 1942–6, perfect English, never so much as met his father, no bitterness. Brought up exclusively by the first Frau Mannheim, actress. He showed me a still. Kohled eyes, expressionist cheekbones, star of Mannheim's UFA one-reeler of *The Fall of the House of Usher*, now lost. Frau von Mannheim, victim of the Dresden fire raid. Hm. Her son expressed no bitterness at that, either, and I felt ashamed until he told me she'd ended up the official mistress of a fairly nasty Nazi. Then I felt better.

I'd actually got to meet the second Mrs Mann, now a retired office cleaner and full-time lush in downtown LA. Once a starlet; lack of exposure terminated her career. Once a call girl. Age terminated her career. The years had dealt hardly with her. Vaguely, she recalled him, a man she once married. She'd had a hangover, he moved into her apartment. She'd still had a hangover. Then he moved out. *God*, she'd had a hangover. They divorced and she married somebody else, whose name escaped her. She accepted ten bucks off me with the negligent grace of habitual custom. I couldn't think why he'd married her and she couldn't remember.

Anyway, after I'd donated ten bucks and packed up my tape recorder, she, as if now I'd paid she felt she owed, started to rummage around amongst the cardboard boxes – shoe boxes, wine crates – with which her one-room competency was mostly furnished. Things tipped and slithered everywhere, satin dancing slippers, old hats, artificial flowers; spilled face powder rose up in clouds and out of the clouds, she, wheezing with triumph, emerged with a photograph.

Nothing so quaint as out-of-date porn. It was an artfully posed spanking pic. I knew him at once, with his odd, soft, pale, malleable face, the blond, slicked-down hair, the moustache, in spite of the gym slip, suspenders and black silk stockings; he sprawled athwart the knee of the second Mrs Mann, who sported a long-line leather bra and splendid boots. Hand raised ready to smack his exposed botty, she turned upon the camera a toothy smile. She'd been quite pretty, in a spit-curled way. She said I could have the snap for a couple of hundred dollars but I was on a tight budget and thought it wouldn't add much to the history of film.

Foresightfully, von Mannheim had left Germany in good time, but he started over in Hollywood at the bottom (forgive the double entendre). His ascent, however, was brisk. Assistant art director, assistant director, director.

The masterpiece of Mann's Hollywood period is, of course, *Paracelsus* (1937), with Charles Laughton. Laughton's great bulk swims into pools of scalding light out of greater or lesser shoals of darkness like a vast monster of the deep, a great, black whale. The movie haunts you like a bad dream. Mann did not try to give you a sense of the past; instead, *Paracelsus* looks as if it had been made in the middle ages – the gargoyle faces, bodies warped with ague, gaunt with famine, a claustrophobic sense of a limited world, of chronic, cramped unfreedom.

The Spirit of Cinema cameos in *Paracelsus* as the Gnostic goddess of wisdom, Sophia, in a kind of Rosicrucian sabbat scene. They were married, by then. Mann wanted his new bride nude for this sabbat, which caused a stir at the time and eventually he was forced to shoot only her disembodied face floating above suggestive shadow. Suggestive, indeed; from his piece of sleight of hand sprang two myths, one easily discredited by aficionados of the rest of her oeuvre, that she had the biggest knockers in the business, the other, less easily dismissed, that she was thickly covered with body hair from the sternum to the knee. Even Mann's exassistant director believed the latter. 'Furry as a spider,' he characterised her. 'And just as damn lethal.' I'd smuggled a half-pint of Jack Daniels into his geriatric ward; he waxed virulent, he warned me to take a snake-bite kit to the interview.

Paracelsus was, needless to say, one of the greatest box-office disasters in the history of the movies. Plans were shelved for his long-dreamed-of *Faust*, with the Spirit either as Gretchen or as Mephistopheles, or as Gretchen doubling *with* Mephistopheles, depending on what he said in different interviews. Mann was forced to perpetrate a hack job, a wallowing melo with the Spirit as twins, a good girl in a blonde wig and a bad girl in a black one, from which his career never recovered and her own survival truly miraculous.

Shortly after this notorious stinker was released to universal jeers, he did the *A Star is Born* bit, although he walked, not into the sea, but into the very swimming pool, that one over there, in which his relict now disposes of her glassware.

As for the Spirit, she found a new director, was rumoured to have undergone a little, a very little plastic surgery, and, the next year, won her first Oscar. From that time on, she was unstoppable, though always she carried her tragedy with her, like a permanent widow's veil, giving her the spooky allure of a born-again *princesse lointaine*.

Who liked to keep her guests waiting.

In my nervous ennui, I cast my eyes round and round the terrace until I came upon something passing strange in the moist earth of a flowerbed.

Moist, therefore freshly watered, though not by whatever it was had left such amazing spoor behind it. No big-game hunter I, but I could have sworn that, impressed on the soil, as if in fresh concrete outside Graumann's Chinese

Theatre, was the print, unless the tiger lilies left it, of a large, clawed paw.

Did you know a lion's mane grows grey with age? I didn't. But the geriatric feline that now emerged from a clump of something odorous beneath the cryptomeria had snow all over his hairy eaves. He appeared as taken aback to see me as I was to bump into him. Our eyes locked. Face like a boxer with a broken nose. Then he tilted his enormous head to one side, opened his mouth – God, his breath was foul – and roared like the last movement of Beethoven's Ninth. With a modest blow of a single paw, he could have batted me arse over tip off the cliff half-way to Hawaii. I wouldn't say it was much comfort to see he'd had his teeth pulled out.

'Aw, come on, Pussy, he don't want to be gummed to death,' said a cracked, harsh, aged, only residually female voice. 'Go fetch Mama, now, there's a good boy.'

The lion grumbled a little in his throat but trotted off into the house with the most touching obedience and I took breath, again – I noticed I'd somehow managed not to for some little time – and sank into one of the white metal terrace chairs. My poor heart was going pit-a-pat, I can tell you, but the *personnage* who had at last appeared from somewhere in the darkening compound neither apologised for nor expressed concern about my nasty shock. She stood there, arms akimbo, surveying me with a satirical, piercing, blue eye.

Except for the jarring circumstance that in one hand she held a stainless steel, many-branched candlestick of awesomely chaste design, she looked like a superannuated lumberjack, plaid skirt, blue jeans, workboots, butch leather belt with a giant silver skull and crossbones for a buckle, coarse, cropped, grey hair escaping from a red bandana tied Indian-style around her head. Her skin was

wrinkled in pinpricks like the surface of parmesan cheese
and a putty grey in colour.

'You the one that's come about the thesis?' she queried.
Her diction was pure hillbilly.

I burbled in the affirmative.

'He's come about the thesis,' she repeated to herself
sardonically and discomforted me still further by again
cackling to herself.

But now an ear-splitting roar announced action was
about to commence. This Ma, or Pa, Kettle person set down
her candlestick on the terrace table, briskly struck a match
on the seat of her pants and applied the flame to the wicks,
dissipating the gathering twilight as She rolled out the
door. Rolled. She sat in a chrome and ivory leather wheelchair as if upon a portable throne. Her right hand rested
negligently on the lion's mane. She was a sight to see.

How long had she spent dressing up for the interview?
Hours. Days. Weeks. She had on a white satin bias-cut
lace-trimmed negligée circa 1935, her skin had that sugar
almond, one hundred per cent Max Factor look and she
wore what I assumed was a wig due to the unnatural
precision of the snowy curls. Only she'd gone too far with
the wig; it gave her a Medusa look. Her mouth looked
funny because her lips had disappeared with age so all that
was left was a painted-in red trapezoid.

But she didn't look her age, at all, at all – oh, no; she
looked a good ten or fifteen years younger, though I doubt
the vision of a sexy septuagenarian was the one for which
she'd striven as she decked herself out. Impressive, though.
Impressive as hell.

And you knew at once this was the face that launched
a thousand ships. Not because anything lovely was still
smouldering away in those old bones; she'd, as it were,
transcended beauty. But something in the way she held her

head, some imperious arrogance, demanded that you look at her and keep on looking.

At once I went into automatic, I assumed the stance of gigolo. I picked up her hand, kissed it, said: '*Enchanté*,' bowed. Had I not been wearing sneakers, I'd have clicked my heels. The Spirit appeared pleased but not surprised by this, but she couldn't smile for fear of cracking her make-up. She whispered me a throaty greeting, eyeing me in a very peculiar way, a way that made the look in the lion's eye seem positively vegetarian.

It freaked me. She freaked me. It was her *star quality*. So *that's* what they mean! I thought. I'd never before, nor am I likely to again, encountered such psychic force as streamed out of that frail little old lady in her antique lingerie and her wheelchair. And, yes, there was something undeniably erotic about it, although she was old as the hills; it was as though she got the most extraordinary sexual charge from being looked at and this charge bounced back on the looker, as though some mechanism inside herself converted your regard into sexual energy. I wondered, not quite terrified, if I was for it, know what I mean.

And all the time I kept thinking, it kept running through my head: 'The phantom is up from the cellars again!'

Night certainly brought out the scent of jasmine.

She whispered me a throaty greeting. Her faded voice meant you had to crouch to hear her, so her cachou-flavoured breath stung your cheek, and you could tell she loved to make you crouch.

'My sister,' she husked, gesturing towards the lumberjack lady who was watching this performance of domination and submission with her thumbs stuck in her belt and an expression of unrelieved cynicism on her face. Her sister. God.

The lion rubbed its head against my leg, making me jump, and she pummelled its graying mane.

'And this – oh! you'll have seen him a thousand times; more exposure than any of us. Allow me to introduce Leo, formerly of MGM.'

The old beast cocked its head from side to side and roared again, in unmistakable fashion, as if to identify itself. Mickey Mouse does her chauffeuring. Every morning, she takes a ride on Trigger.

'*Ars gratia artis*,' she reminded me, as if guessing my thoughts. 'Where could he go, poor creature, when they retired him? Nobody would touch a fallen star. So he came right here, to live with Mama, didn't you, darling.'

'Drinkies!' announced Sister, magnificently clattering a welcome, bottle-laden trolley.

After the third poolside martini, which was gin at which a lemon briefly sneered, I judged it high time to broach the subject of Hank Mann. It was pitch dark by then, a few stars burning, night sounds, sea sounds, the creak of those metal chairs that seemed to have been designed, probably on purpose, by the butch sister, to break your balls. But it was difficult to get a word in. The Spirit was briskly checking out my knowledge of screen history.

'No, the art director certainly was *not* Ben Carré, how absurd to think that! . . . My goodness me, young man, Wallace Reid was dead and buried by then, and good riddance to bad rubbish . . . Edith Head? Edith Head design Nancy Carroll's patent leather evening dress? Who put that into your noddle?'

Now and then the lion sandpapered the back of my hand with its tongue, as if to show sympathy. The butch sister put away gin by the tumblerful, two to my one, and creaked resonantly from time to time, like an old door.

'No, no, no, young man! Laughton certainly was *not* addicted to self-abuse!'

And out of the dark it came to me that that dreamy perfume of jasmine issued from no flowering shrub but, instead, right out of the opening sequence of *Double Indemnity*, do you remember? And I suffered a ghastly sense of incipient humiliation, of impending erotic doom, so that I shivered, and Sister, alert and either comforting or complicitous, sloshed another half pint of gin into my glass.

Then Sister belched and announced: 'Gonna take a leak.'

Evidently equipped with night vision, she rolled off into the gloaming from whence, after a pause, came the tinkle of running water. She'd gone back to Nature as far as toilet training was concerned, cut out the frills. The raunchy sound of Sister making pee-pee brought me down to earth again. I clutched my tumbler, for the sake of holding something solid.

'About thish time,' I said, 'you met Hank Mann.'

Night and candlelight turned the red mouth black, but her satin dress shone like water with plankton in it.

'Heinrich,' she corrected with a click of orthodontics; and then, or so it seemed, fell directly into a trance for, all at once, she fixed her gaze on the middle distance and said no more.

I thankfully took advantage of her lapse of attention to pour my gin down the side of my chair, trusting that by the morrow it would be indistinguishable from lion piss. Sister, clanking her death's-head belt-buckle as she readjusted her clothing, came back to us and juggled ice and lemon slices as if nothing untoward was taking place. Then, in a perfectly normal, even conversational tone, the

Spirit said: 'White kisses, red kisses. And coke in a golden casket on top of the baby grand. Those were the days.'

Sister t'sked, possibly with irritation.

'Reckon you've had a skinful,' said Sister. 'Reckon you deserve a stiff whupping.'

That roused the Spirit somewhat, who chuckled and lunged at the gin which, fortunately, stood within her reach. She poured a fresh drink down the hatch in a matter of seconds, then made a vague gesture with her left hand, inadvertently biffing the lion in the ear. The lion had dozed off and grumbled like an empty stomach to have his peace disturbed.

'They wore away her face by looking at it too much. So we made her a new one.'

'Hee haw, hee haw,' said Sister. She was not braying but laughing.

The Spirit propped herself on the arm of her wheelchair and pierced me with a look. Something told me we had gone over some kind of edge. Nancy Carroll's evening dress, indeed. Enough of that nonsense. Now we were on a different plane.

'I used to think of prayer wheels,' she informed me. 'Night after night, prayer wheels ceaselessly turning in the darkened cathedrals, those domed and gilded palaces of the Faith, the Majestics, the Rialtos, the Alhambras, those grottoes of the miraculous in which the creatures of the dream came out to walk within the sight of men. And the wheels spun out those subtle threads of light that wove the liturgies of that reverential age, the last great age of religion. While the wonderful people out there in the dark, the congregation of the faithful, the company of the blessed, they leant forward, they aspired upwards, they imbibed the transmission of divine light.

'Now, the priest is he who prints the anagrams of desire

upon the stock; but whom does he project upon the universe? Another? Or, himself?'

All this was somewhat more than I'd bargained for. I fought with the gin fumes reeling in my head, I needed all my wits about me. Moment by moment, she became more gnomic. Surreptitiously, I fumbled with my briefcase. I wanted to get that tape-recorder spooling away, didn't I; why, it might have been Mannheim talking.

'Is he the one who interprets the spirit or does the spirit speak through him? Or is he only, all the time, nothing but the merchant of shadows?

'Hic,' she interrupted herself.

Then Sister, whose vision was not one whit impaired by time or liquor, extended her trousered leg in one succinct and noiseless movement and kicked my briefcase clear into the pool, where it dropped with a liquid plop.

In spite of the element of poetic justice in it, that my file on Mannheim should suffer the same fate as he, I must admit that now I fell into a great fear. I even thought they might have lured me here to murder me, this siren of the cinema and her weird acolyte. Remember, they had made me quite drunk; it was a moonless night and I was far from home; and I was trapped helpless among these beings who could only exist in California, where the light made movies and madness. And one of them had just arbitrarily drowned the poor little tools of my parasitic trade, leaving me naked and at their mercy. The kindly lion shook himself awake and licked my hand again, perhaps to reassure me, but I wasn't expecting it and jumped half out of my skin.

The Spirit broke into speech again.

'She is only in semi-retirement, you know. She still spends three hours every morning looking through the scripts that almost break the mailman's back as he staggers beneath them up to her cliff-top retreat.

'Age does not wither her; we've made quite sure of that, young man. She still irradiates the dark, for did we not discover the true secret of immortality together? How to exist almost and only in the eye of the beholder, like a genuine miracle?'

I cannot say it comforted me to theorise this lady was, to some degree, possessed, and so was perfectly within her rights to refer to herself in the third person in that ventriloqual, insubstantial voice that scratched the ear as smoke scratches the back of the throat. But by whom or what possessed? I felt very close to the perturbed spirit of Heinrich von Mannheim and the metaphysics of the Great Art of Light and Shade, I can tell you. And speaking of the latter – Athanias Kircher, author, besides, of *Spectacula Paradoxa Rerum* (1624), *The Universal Theatre of Paradoxes*.

Her eyelids were drooping now, and as they closed her mouth fell open, but she spoke no more.

The Sister broke the silence as if it were wind.

'That's about the long and short of it, young man,' she said. 'Got enough for your thesis?'

She heaved herself up with a sigh so huge that, horrors! it blew out all the candles and then, worse and worse! she left me alone with the Spirit. But nothing more transpired because the Spirit seemed to have passed, if not on, then out, flat out in her wheelchair, and the inner light that brought out the shine on her satin dress was extinguished too. I saw nothing, until a set of floods concealed in the pines around us came on and everything was visible as common daylight, the old lady, the drowsing lion, the depleted drinks trolley, the slices of lemon ground into the terrace by my nervous feet, the little plants pushing up between the cracks in the paving, the black water of the swimming-pool in which my over-excited, suddenly light-wounded senses hallucinated a corpse.

Which last resolved itself, as I peered, headachy and blinking, into my own briefcase, opened, spilling out a floating debris of papers and tape boxes. I poured myself another gin, to steady my nerves. Sister appeared again, right behind my shoulder, making me jog my elbow so gin soaked my jeans. Her Indian headband had knocked rakishly askew, giving her a piratical air. In close-up, her bones, clearly visible under her ruined skin, reminded me of somebody else's, but I was too chilled, drunk and miserable to care whose they might be. She was cackling to herself, again.

'We hates y'all with the tape recorders,' she said. 'Reckon us folks thinks you is dancin' on our graves.'

She aimed a foot at the brake on the Spirit's wheelchair and briskly pushed it and its unconscious contents into the house. The lion woke up, yawned like the opening of the San Andreas fault and padded after. The sliding door slid to. After a moment, a set of concealing crimson curtains swished along the entire length of the glass wall and that was that. I half-expected to see the words, THE END, come up on the curtains, but then the lights went off and I was in the dark.

Unwilling to negotiate the crazy steps down to the gate, I reached sightlessly for the gin and sucked it until I fell into a troubled slumber.

And I awoke me on the cold hill-side.

Well, not exactly. I woke up to find myself tucked into the back seat of my own VW, parked on the cliff beside the Toyota truck in the grey hour before dawn, my frontal lobes and all my joints a-twang with pain. I didn't even try the gate of the house. I got out of the car, shook myself, got back in again and headed straight home. After a while, on the perilous road to the freeway, I saw in the driving mirror a vehicle approaching me from behind. It was the red Toyota truck. Sister, of course, at the wheel.

She overtook me at illicit speed, blasting the horn joyously, waving with one hand, her face split in a toothless grin. When I saw that smile, even though the teeth were missing, I knew who she reminded me of – of a girl in a dirndl on a cardboard alp, smiling because at last she saw approaching her the man who would release her . . . If I hadn't, in the interests of scholarship, sat yawning through that dire operetta in the viewing booth, I would never have so much as guessed.

She must have hated the movies. Hated them. She had the lion in back. They looked as if they were enjoying the ride. Probably Leo had smiled for the cameras once too often, too. They parked at the place where the cliff road ended and waited there, quite courteously, until I was safely embarked among the heavy morning traffic, out of their lives.

How had they found a corpse to substitute for Mannheim? A corpse was never the most difficult thing to come by in Southern California, I suppose. I wondered if, after all those years, they finally decided to let me in on the masquerade. And, if so, why.

Perhaps, having constructed this masterpiece of subterfuge, Mannheim couldn't bear to die without leaving some little hint, somewhere, of how, having made her, he then *became* her, became a better she than she herself had ever been, and wanted to share with his last little acolyte, myself, the secret of his greatest hit. But, more likely, he simply couldn't resist turning himself into the Spirit one last time, couldn't let down his public . . . for they weren't to know I'd seen a picture of him in a frock, already, were they, although in those days, he still wore a moustache. And that clinched it, in my own mind, when I remembered the second Mrs Mann's spanking picture, although this conviction did not make me any the less ill at ease.

In the healthfood restaurant, Hiroko slapped the carrot-juicer with a filthy cloth and fed me brown rice and chilled bean-curd with chopped onion and ginger on top, pursing her lips with distaste; she herself only ate Kentucky fried chicken. Business was slack in the mid-afternoon and I wanted her to come upstairs with me for a while, to remind me there was more to flesh than light and illusion, but she shook her head.

'Boring,' she said, offensively. After a while she added, though in no conciliatory tone, 'Not just you. Everything. California. I've seen this movie. I'm going home.'

'I thought you said you felt like an enemy alien at home, Hiroko.'

She shrugged, staring through her midnight bangs at the white sunlight outside.

'Better the devil you know,' she said.

I realised I was just a wild oat to her, a footnote to her trip, and, although she had been just the same to me, all the same I grew glum to realise how peripheral I was, and suddenly wanted to go home, too, and longed for rain again, and television, that secular medium.

PART TWO

The Ghost Ships

A Christmas Story

————

Therefore that whosoever shall be found observing any
such day as Christmas or the like, either by forbearing of
labor, feasting, or any other way upon any such account
aforesaid, every person so offending shall pay for every
offense five shillings as a fine to the county.

*Statute enacted by the General Court of
Massachusetts, May 1659, repealed 1681*

'Twas the night before Christmas. Silent night, holy night.
The snow lay deep and crisp and even. Etc. etc. etc.; let
these familiar words conjure up the traditional anticipatory
magic of Christmas Eve, and then – forget it.

Forget it. Even if the white moon above Boston Bay
ensures that all is calm, all is bright, there will be no Christmas *as such* in the village on the shore that now lies locked
in a precarious winter dream.

(Dream, that uncensorable state. They would forbid it if
they could.)

At that time, for we are talking about a long time ago,
about three and a quarter hundred years ago, the newcomers had no more than scribbled their signatures on the
blank page of the continent that was, as it lay under the
snow, no whiter nor more pure than their intentions.

They plan to write more largely; they plan to inscribe
thereon the name of God.

And that was why, because of their awesome piety, tomorrow, on Christmas Day, they will wake, pray and go about their business as if it were any other day.

For them, all days are holy but none are holidays.

New England is the new leaf they have just turned over; Old England is the dirty linen their brethren at home have just – did they not recently win the English Civil War? – washed in public. Back home, for the sake of spiritual integrity, their brothers and sisters have broken the graven images in the churches, banned the playhouses where men dress up as women, chopped down the village Maypoles because they welcome in the spring in altogether too orgiastic a fashion.

Nothing particularly radical about that, given the Puritans' basic premises. Anyone can see at a glance that a Maypole, proudly erect upon the village green as the sap is rising, is a godless instrument. The very thought of Cotton Mather, with blossom in his hair, dancing round the Maypole makes the imagination reel. No. The greatest genius of the Puritans lay in their ability to sniff out a pagan survival in, say, the custom of decorating a house with holly for the festive season; they were the stuff of which social anthropologists would be made!

And their distaste for the icon of the lovely lady with her bonny babe – Mariolatry. graven images! – is less subtle than their disgust at the very idea of the festive season itself. It was the *festivity* of it that irked them.

Nevertheless, it assuredly *is* a gross and heathenish practice, to welcome the birth of Our Saviour with feasting, drunkenness, and lewd displays of mumming and masquerading.

We want none of that filth in this new place.

No, thank you.

*

As midnight approached, the cattle in the byres lumbered down upon their knees in homage, according to the well-established custom of over sixteen hundred English winters when they had mimicked the kneeling cattle in the Bethlehem stable; then, remembering where they were in the nick of time, they hastily refrained from idolatry and hauled themselves upright.

Boston Bay, calm as milk, black as ink, smooth as silk. And, suddenly, at just the hour when the night spins on its spindle and starts to unravel its own darkness, at what one could call, elsewhere, the witching hour –

> I saw three ships come sailing in,
> Christmas Day, Christmas Day,
> I saw three ships come sailing in
> On Christmas Day in the morning.

Three ships, silent as ghost ships; ghost ships of Christmas past.

And what was in those ships all three?

Not, as in the old song, 'the Virgin Mary and her baby'; that would have done such grievous damage to the history of the New World that you might not be reading this in the English language even. No; the imagination must obey the rules of actuality. (Some of them, anyway.)

Therefore I imagine that the first ship was green and leafy all over, built of mossy Yule logs bound together with ivy. It was loaded to the gunwales with roses and pomegranates, the flower of Mary and the fruit that represents her womb, and the mast was a towering cherry tree which, now and then, leaned down to scatter ripe fruit on the water in memory of the carol that nobody in New England now sang. The Cherry Tree Carol, that tells how, when Mary asked Joseph to pick her some cherries, he was jealous and spiteful and told her to ask the father of her unborn child to help her pick them – and, at that, the cherry tree bowed down so low the cherries dangled in her lap, almost.

Clinging to the mast of this magic cherry tree was an abundance of equally inadmissible mistletoe, sacred since the dawn of time, when the Druids used to harvest it with silver sickles before going on to perform solstitial rites of memorable beastliness at megalithic sites all over Europe.

Yet more mistletoe dangled from the genial bundle of evergreens, the kissing bough, that invitation to the free exchange of precious bodily fluids.

And what is that bunch of holly, hung with red apples and knots of red ribbon? Why, it is a wassail bob.

This is what you did with your wassail bob. You carried it to the orchard with you when you took out a jar of hard cider to give the apple trees their Christmas drink. All over Somerset, all over Dorset, everywhere in the apple-scented cider country of Old England, time out of mind, they souse the apple trees at Christmas, get them good and drunk, soak them.

You pour the cider over the tree trunks, let it run down to the roots. You fire off guns, you cheer, you shout. You serenade the future apple crop and next year's burgeoning, you 'wassail' them, you toast their fecundity in last year's juices.

But not in *this* village. If a sharp smell of fruit and greenery wafted from the leafy ship to the shore, refreshing their dreams, all the same, the immigration officials at the front of the brain, the port of entry for memory, sensed contraband in the incoming cargo and snapped: 'Permission to land refused!'

There was a furious silent explosion of green leaves, red berries, white berries, of wet, red seeds from bursting pomegranates, of spattering cherries and scattering flowers; and cast to the winds and scattered was the sappy, juicy, voluptuous flesh of all the wood demons, tree spirits and fertility goddesses who had ever, once upon a time, contrived to hitch a ride on Christmas.

Then the ship and all it had contained were gone.

But the second ship now began to belch forth such a savoury aroma from a vent amidships that the most abstemious dreamer wrinkled his nose with pleasure. This ship rode low in the water, for it was built in the unmistakable shape of a pie dish and, as it neared shore, it could be seen that the deck itself was made of piecrust just out of the oven, glistening with butter, gilded with egg yolk.

Not a ship at all, in fact, but a Christmas pie!

But now the piecrust heaved itself up to let tumbling out into the water a smoking cargo of barons of beef gleaming with gravy, swans upon spits and roast geese dripping hot fat. And the figurehead of this jolly vessel was a boar's head, wreathed in bay, garlanded in rosemary, a roasted apple in its mouth and sprigs of rosemary tucked behind its ears. Above, hovered a pot of mustard, with wings.

Those were hungry days in the new-found land. The floating pie came wallowing far closer in than the green ship had done, close enough for the inhabitants of the houses on the foreshore to salivate in their sleep.

But then, with one accord, they recalled that burnt offerings and pagan sacrifice of pig, bird and cattle could never be condoned. In unison, they rolled over on to their other sides and turned their stern backs.

The ship span round once, then twice. Then, the mustard pot swooping after, it dove down to the bottom of the sea, leaving behind a bobbing mass of sweetmeats that dissipated itself gradually, like sea wrack, leaving behind only a single cannonball of the plum-packed Christmas pudding of Old England that the sea's omnivorous belly found too much, too indigestible, and rejected it, so that the pudding refused to sink.

The sleepers, freed from the ghost not only of gluttony but also of dyspepsia, sighed with relief.

Now there was only one ship left.

The silence of the dream lent this apparition an especial eeriness.

This last ship was packed to the gunwales with pagan survivals of the most concrete kind, the ones in – roughly – human shape. The masts and spars were hung with streamers, paperchains and balloons, but the gaudy decorations were almost hidden by the motley crew of queer types aboard, who would have been perfectly visible from the shore in every detail of their many-coloured fancy dress had anyone been awake to see them.

Reeling to and fro on the deck, tumbling and dancing, were all the mummers and masquers and Christmas dancers that Cotton Mather hated so, every one of them large as life and twice as unnatural. The rouged men dressed as women, with pillowing bosoms; the clog dancers, making a soundless rat-a-tat-tat on the boards with their wooden shoes; the sword dancers whacking their wooden blades and silently jingling the little bells on their ankles. All these riotous revellers used to welcome in the festive season back home; it was they who put the 'merry' into Merry England!

And now, horrors! they sailed nearer and nearer the sanctified shore, as if intent on forcing the saints to celebrate Christmas whether they wanted to or no.

The saint the Church disowned, Saint George, was there, in paper armour painted silver, with his old foe, the Turkish knight, a chequered tablecloth tied round his head for a turban, fencing with clubs as they used to every Christmas in the Old Country, going from house to house with the mumming play that was rooted far more deeply in antiquity than the birth it claimed to celebrate.

This is the plot of the mumming play: Saint George and the Turkish knight fight until Saint George knocks the Turkish knight down. In comes the Doctor, with his black bag, and brings him back to life again – a shocking mockery of death and resurrection. (Or else a ritual of revivification, depending on one's degree of faith, and also, of course, depending on one's degree of faith in what.)

The master of these floating revels was the Lord of Misrule himself, the clown prince of Old Christmas, to which he came from fathoms deep in time. His face was blackened with charcoal. A calf's tail was stitched on to the rump of his baggy pants, which constantly fell down, to be hitched up again after a glimpse of his hairy buttocks. His top hat sported paper roses. He carried an inflated bladder with which he merrily battered the dancing heads around him. He was a true antique, as old as the festival that existed at midwinter before Christmas was ever thought of. Older.

His descendants live, all year round, in the circus. He is mirth, anarchy and terror. Father Christmas is his bastard son, whom he has disowned for not being obscene enough.

The Lord of Misrule was there when the Romans

celebrated the Winter Solstice, the hinge on which the year turns. The Romans called it Saturnalia and let the slaves rule the roost for the duration, when all was topsy-turvy and almost everything that occurred would have been illegal in the Commonwealth of Massachusetts at the time of the ghost ships, if not today.

Yet from the phantom festival on the bedizened deck came the old, old message: during the twelve days of Christmas, nothing is forbidden, everything is forgiven.

A merry Christmas is Cotton Mather's worst nightmare.

If a little merriment imparts itself to the dreams of the villagers, they do not experience it as pleasure. They have exorcised the vegetables, and the slaughtered beasts; they will not tolerate, here, the riot of unreason that used to mark, over there, the inverted season of the year when nights are longer than days and the rivers do not run and you think that when the sun sinks over the rim of the sea it might never come back again.

The village raised a silent cry: Avaunt thee! Get thee hence!

The riotous ship span round once, twice – a third time. And then sank, taking its Dionysiac crew with it.

But, just as he was about to be engulfed, the Lord of Misrule caught hold of the Christmas pudding that still floated on the water. This Christmas pudding, sprigged with holly, stuffed with currants, raisins, almonds, figs, compressed all the Christmas contraband into one fearful sphere.

The Lord of Misrule drew back his arm and bowled the pudding towards the shore.

Then he, too, went down. The Atlantic gulped him. The moon set, the snow came down again and it was a night like any other winter night.

Except, next morning, before dawn, when all rose to pray in the shivering dark, the little children, thrusting their feet reluctantly into their cold shoes, found a juicy resistance to the progress of their great toes and, investigating further, discovered to their amazed and secret glee, each child a raisin the size of your thumb, wrinkled with its own sweetness, plump as if it had been soaked in brandy, that came from who knows where but might easily have dropped out of the sky during the flight overhead of a disintegrating Christmas pudding.

In Pantoland

'I'm bored with television,' announced Widow Twankey from her easy chair in the Empyrean, switching off *The Late Show* and adjusting his/her falsies inside her outrageous red bustier. 'I will descend again to Pantoland!'

> In Pantoland,
> Everything is grand.

Well, let's not exaggerate – grandish. Not like what it used to be but, then, what is. Even so, all still brightly coloured – garish, in fact, all your primaries, red, yellow, blue. And all excessive, so that your castle has more turrets than a regular castle, your forest is considerably more impenetrable than the average forest and, not infrequently, your cow has more than its natural share of teats and udders. We're talking multiple projections, here, spikes, sprouts, boobs, bums. It's a bristling world, in Pantoland, either phallic or else demonically, aggressively female and there's something archaic behind it all, archaic in the worst sense. Something positively filthy.

But all also two-dimensional, so that Maid Marian's house, in Pantoland's fictive Nottingham, is flat as a pancake. The front door may well open when she goes in, but it makes a hollow sound behind her when she slams it shut and the entire façade gets the shivers. Robin serenades her from below; she opens her window to riposte and what you see behind her of her bedroom is only a painted bedhead on a painted wall.

Of course, the real problem here is that it is Baron Hardup of Hardup Hall, father of Cinderella, stepfather of the Ugly Sisters, who, these barren days, all too often occupies the post of Minister of Finance in Pantoland. Occasionally, even now, the free-spenders such as Princess Badroulbador take things into their own hands and then you get some wonderful effects, such as a three-masted galleon in full sail breasting through tumultuous storms with thunder booming and lightning breaking about the spars as the gallant ship takes Dick Whittington and his cat either away from or else back to London amidst a nostalgic series of *tableaux vivants* of British naval heroes such as Raleigh, Drake, Captain Cook and Nelson, discovering things or keeping the Channel safe for English shipping, while Dick gives out a full-throated contralto rendition of 'If I had a hammer' with a chorus of rats in masks and tights, courtesy of the Italia Conti school.

Illusion and transformation, kitchen into palace with the aid of gauze etc. etc. etc. You know the kind of thing. It all costs money. And, sometimes, as if it were the greatest illusion of all, there might be an incursion of the real. Real horses, perhaps, trotting, neighing and whinnying, large as life. Yet 'large as life' isn't the right phrase, at all, at all. 'Large as life' they might be, in the context of the auditorium, but when the proscenium arch gapes as wide as the mouth of the ogre in *Jack and the Beanstalk*, those forty white horses pulling the glass coach of the princess look as little and inconsequential as white mice. They are real, all right, but insignificant, and only raise a laugh or round of applause if one of them inadvertently drops dung.

And sometimes there'll be a dog, often one of those sandy-coloured, short-haired terriers. On the programme, it will say: 'Chuckles, played by himself,' just above where it says: 'Cigarettes by Abdullah.' (Whatever happened to Abdullah?) Chuckles does everything they taught him at dog-school – fetches, carries, jumps through a flaming hoop – but now and then he forgets his script, forgets he lives in Pantoland, remembers he is a real dog precipitated into a wondrous world of draughts and pungency and rustlings. He will run down to the footlights, he will look out over the daisy field of upturned, expectant faces and, after a moment's puzzlement, give a little questioning bark.

It was not like this when Toto dropped down into Oz; it is more like it was when Toto landed back, alas, in Kansas. Chuckles does not like it. Chuckles feels let down.

Then Robin Hood or Prince Charming or whoever it is has the titular – and 'tits' is the operative word with this one – ownership of Chuckles in Pantoland, scoops him up against her bosom and he has been saved. He has returned to Pantoland. In Pantoland, he can live for ever.

In Pantoland, which is the carnival of the unacknowledged and the fiesta of the repressed, everything is excessive and gender is variable.

A Brief Look at the Citizens of Pantoland

THE DAME

Double-sexed and self-sufficient, the Dame, the sacred transvestite of Pantoland, manifests him/herself in a number of guises. For example he/she might introduce him/herself thus:

'My name is Widow Twankey.' Then sternly adjure the audience: 'Smile when you say that!'

Because Twankey rhymes with – pardon me, vicar; and,

> Once upon a distant time,
> They talked in Pantoland in rhyme . . .

but now they talk in double entendre, which is a language all its own and is accented, not with the acute or grave, but with the eyebrows. Double entendre. That is, everyday discourse which has been dipped in the infinite riches of a dirty mind.

She/he stars as Mother Goose. In *Cinderella*, you get two for the price of one with the Ugly Sisters. If they throw in Cinders' stepmother, that's a bonanza, that's three. Then there is Jack's Mum in *Jack and the Beanstalk* where the presence of cow and stem in close proximity rams home the 'phallic mother' aspect of the Dame. The Queen of Hearts (who stole some tarts). Granny in *Red Riding Hood*, where the wolf – 'Ooooer!' – gobbles her up. He/she pops up everywhere in Pantoland, tittering and squealing: 'Look out, girls! There's a man!!!' whenever the Principal Boy (q.v.) appears.

Big wigs and round spots of rouge on either cheek and eyelashes longer than those of Daisy the Cow; crinolines that dip and sway and support a mass of crispy petticoats out of which comes running Chuckles the Dog dragging behind him a string of sausages plucked, evidently, from the Dame's fundament.

'Better out than in.'

He/she bestrides the stage. His/her enormous footsteps resonate with the antique past. She brings with him the sacred terror inherent in those of his/her avatars such as Lisa Maron, the androgynous god-goddess of the Abomey pantheon; the great god Shango, thunder deity of the Yorubas, who can be either male or female; the sacrificial priest who, in the Congo, dressed like a woman and was called 'Grandma'.

The Dame bends over, whips up her crinolines; she has three pairs of knee-length bloomers, which she wears according to mood.

One pair of bloomers is made out of the Union Jack, for the sake of patriotism.

The second pair of bloomers is quartered red and black, in memory of Utopia.

The third and vastest pair of bloomers is scarlet, with a target on the seat, centred on the arsehole, and *this* pair is wholly dedicated to obscenity.

Roars. Screams. Hoots.

She turns and curtsies. And what do you know, she/he has shoved a truncheon down her trousers, hasn't she?

In Burgundy, in the Middle Ages, they held a Feast of Fools that lasted all through the dead days, that vacant lapse of time during which, according to the hairy-legged mythology of the Norsemen, the sky wolf ate up the sun. By the time the sky wolf puked it up again, a person or persons unknown had fucked the New Year back into being during the days when all the boys wore sprigs of mistletoe in their hats. Filthy work, but *somebody* had to do it. By the fourteenth century, the far-from-hairy-legged Burgundians had forgotten all about the sky wolf, of course; but had they also forgotten the orgiastic non-time of the Solstice, which, once upon a time, was also the time of the Saturnalia, the topsy-turvy time, 'the Liberties of December', when master swapped places with slave and anything could happen?

The mid-winter carnival in Old Burgundy, known as the Feast of Fools, was reigned over in style by a man dressed as a woman whom they used to call Mère Folle, Crazy Mother.

Crazy Mother turns round and curtsies. She pulls the truncheon out of her bloomers. All shriek in terrified delight and turn away their eyes. But when the punters dare to look again, they encounter only his/her seraphic smile and, lo and behold! the truncheon has turned into a magic wand.

When Widow Twankey/the Queen of Hearts/Mother Goose taps Daisy the Cow with her wand, Daisy the Cow gives out with a chorus of 'Down by the Old Bull and Bush'.

THE BEASTS

1 *The Goose* in *Mother Goose* is, or so they say, the Hamlet of animal roles, introspective and moody as only a costive bird straining over its egg might be. There is a full gamut of emotion in the Goose role – loyalty and devotion to her mother; joy and delight at her own maternity; heartbreak at loss of egg; fear and trembling at the wide variety of gruesome possibilities which might occur if, in the infinite intercouplings of possible texts which occur all the time in the promiscuity of Pantoland, one story effortlessly segues into another story, so that *Mother Goose* twins up with *Jack and the Beanstalk*, involving an egg-hungry ogre, or with *Robin Hood*, incorporating a goose-hungry Sheriff of Nottingham.

Note that the Goose, like the Dame, is a female role usually, though not always, played by a man. But the Goose does not represent the exaggerated and parodic femininity of Widow Twankey. The Goose's femininity is real. She is all woman. Witness the centrality of the egg in her life. So the Goose deserves an interpreter with the sophisticated technique and empathy for gender of the *onnagata*, the female impersonators of the Japanese Kabuki theatre, who can make you weep at the sadness inherent in the sleeves of a kimono as they quiver with suppressed emotion at a woman's lot.

Because of this, and because she is the prime focus of all attention, the Goose in *Mother Goose* is the premier animal role, even more so than . . .

2 *Dick Whittington's Cat:* Dick Whittington's cat is the Scaramouche of Pantoland, limber, agile, and going on two legs more often than on four to stress his status as intermediary between the world of the animals and our world. If he possesses some of the chthonic ambiguity of all dark messengers between different modes of being, nevertheless he is never less than a perfect valet to his master and hops and skips at Dick's bidding. His is therefore less of a starring role than the Goose, even if his rat-catching activities are central to the action and it is as difficult to imagine Dick without his cat as Morecambe without Wise.

Note that this cat is male almost to a fault, unquestionably a tom-cat, and personated by a man; some things are sacrosanct, even in Pantoland. A tom-cat is maleness personified, whereas . . .

3 *Daisy the Cow* is so female it takes two whole men to represent her, one on his own couldn't hack it. The back legs of the pantomime quadruped are traditionally a thankless task, but the front end gets the chance to indulge in all manner of antics, flirting, flattering, fluttering those endless eyelashes and, sometimes, if the coordination between the two ends is good enough, Daisy does a tap-dance, which makes her massive udder with its many dangling teats dip and sway in the most salacious manner, bringing back home the notion of a basic crudely reproductive female sexuality of which those of us who don't lactate often do

not like to be reminded. (They have lactation, generation all the time in mind in Pantoland.)

This rude femaleness requires two men to mimic it, as I've said; therefore you could call Daisy a Dame, squared.

These three are the principal animal leads in Pantoland, although Mother Hubbard, a free-floating Dame who might turn up in any text, always comes accompanied by her dog but, more often than not, Chuckles gets in on the act here, and *real* animals don't count. Pantomime horses can crop up anywhere and mimic rats are not confined to *Dick Whittington* but inhabit Cinderella's kitchen, even drive her coach; there are mice and lizards too. Birds. You need robins to cover up the Babes in the Wood. Emus, you get sometimes. Ducks. You name it.

When Pantoland was young, and I mean *really* young, before it got stage-struck, in the time of the sky wolf, when fertility festivals filled up those vacant, dark, solstitial days, we used to see no difference between ourselves and the animals. Bruno the Bear and Felix the Cat walked and talked amongst us. We lived with, we loved, we married the animals (*Beauty and the Beast*). The Goose, the Cat and Daisy the Cow have come to us out of the paradise that little children remember, when we thought we could talk to the animals, to remind us how once we knew that the animals were just as human as we were, and that made us more human too.

THE PRINCIPAL BOY

What an armful! She is the grandest thing in Pantoland.

Look at those arms! Look at those thighs! Like tree trunks, but like sexy tree trunks. Her hats are huge and plumed with feathers; her gleaming, exiguous little knicks are made of satin and trimmed with sequins. As Prince Charming, she is a veritable spectacle of pure glamour although, as Jack, her costume might start off a touch more peasant and, as Dick, she needs to look like a London apprentice for a while before she gets to try on that Lord Mayor schmutter. For Robin Hood, she'll wear green; as Aladdin, the East is signified by her turban.

You can tell she is supposed to be a man not by her shape, which is a conventional hour-glass, but by her body language. She marches with as martial a stride as it is possible to achieve in stiletto heels and throws out her arms in wide, generous, all-encompassing, patriarchal gestures, as if she owned the earth. Her maleness has an antique charm, even, nowadays, a touch of wistful Edwardiana about it; no Principal Boy worth her salt would want to personate a New Man, after all. She's gone to the bother of turning herself into a Principal Boy to get away from the washing-up, in the first place.

In spite of her spilling physical luxuriance, which ensures that, unlike the more ambivalent Dame, the Principal Boy is always referred to as a 'she', her voice is a deep, dark brown and, when raised in song, could raise the dead. Who, who ever heard her, could ever forget a Principal Boy of the Old School leading the chorus in a rousing military parade and rendition of, say, 'Where are the boys of the Old Brigade?'

Come to that, where *are* the Principal Boys of the Old Brigade? In these anorexic times, there is less and less thigh to slap. Girls, nowadays, are big-bosomed, all right, due to implants, but not deep-chested any more. Principal Boys used to share a hollow-voiced, bass-baritone bonhomie with department-store Father Christmases but 'Ho! ho! ho!' is heard no more in the land. In these lean times, your average Principal Boy looks more like a Peter Pan, and prepubescence isn't what you're aiming for at a fertility festival, although the presence of actual children, in great numbers, laughing at that which they should not know about, is indispensable as having established the success of preceding fertility festivals.

The Principal Boy is a male/female cross, like the Dame, but she is never played for laughs. No. She is played for thrills, for adventure, for romance. So, after innumerable adventures, she ends up with the Principal Girl in a number where their voices soar and swoon together as in the excruciatingly erotic climactic aria of Monteverdi's *L'Incoronazione di Poppaea*, performed as it is in the present day always by two ladies, one playing Nero, one Poppaea, due to male castrati being thin on the ground in spite of the population explosion. And, as Principal Boy and Principal Girl duet, their four breasts in two décolletages jostle one another for pre-eminence in the eyes of all observers. This is a thrill indeed but will not make babies unless they then dash out and borrow the turkey-baster from the Christmas-dinner kitchen. There is a kind of censorship inherent in the pantomime.

But the question of gender remains vague because you have to hang on to the idea that the Principal Boy is all boy and all girl *at the same time*, a door that opens both ways, just as the Dame is Mother Eve and Old Adam in one parcel; they are both doors that open both ways, they are the Janus faces of the season, they look backwards and forwards, they bury the past, they procreate the future, and, by rights, these two should belong together for they are and are not ambivalent and the Principal Girl (q. does *not* v. in this work of reference) is nothing more than a pretty prop, even when eponymous as in *Cinderella* and *Snow White*.

*

Widow Twankey came out of retirement and, gorged on anthropology, dropped down on stage in Pantoland.

'I have come back to earth and I feel randy!'

She/he didn't have to say a word. The décor picked up on her unutterance and all the pasteboard everywhere shuddered.

The Dame and the Principal Boy come together by chance in the Chinese laundry. Aladdin has brought in his washing. They exchange some banter about smalls and drawers, eyeing one another up. They know that this time, for the first time since censorship began, the script will change.

'I feel randy,' said Widow Twankey.

What is a fertility festival without a ritual copulation?

But it isn't as simple as that. For now, oh! now the hobby-horse is quite forgot. The Phallic Mother and the Big-Breasted Boy must take second place in the contemporary cast-list to some cricketer who does not even know enough to make an obscene gesture with his bat, since, in the late twentieth century, the planet is overpopulated and four breasts in harmony is what we need more of, rather than babies, so Widow Twankey ought to go and have it off with Mother Hubbard and stop bothering Aladdin, really she/he ought.

Do people still believe in Pantoland?

If you believe in Pantoland, put your palms together and give a big hand to . . .

If you *really* believe in Pantoland, put your – pardon me, vicar –

A fertility festival without a ritual copulation is . . . nothing but a pantomime.

Widow Twankey has come back to earth to restore the pantomime to its original condition.

*

But, before scarlet drawers and satin knicks could hit the floor, a hook dropped out of the flies and struck Widow Twankey between the shoulders. The hook lodged securely in her red satin bustier; shouting and screaming, with a great display of scrawny shin, she was hauled back up where she had come from, in spite of her raucous protests, and deposited back amongst the dead stars, leaving the Principal Boy at a loss for what to do except to briskly imitate George Formby and start to sing 'Oh, Mr Wu, I'm telling you . . .'

As Umberto Eco once said, 'An everlasting carnival does not work.' You can't keep it up, you know; nobody ever could. The essence of the carnival, the festival, the Feast of Fools, is transience. It is here today and gone tomorrow, a release of tension not a reconstitution of order, a refreshment . . . after which everything can go on again exactly as if nothing had happened.

Things don't change because a girl puts on trousers or a chap slips on a frock, you know. Masters were masters again the day after Saturnalia ended; after the holiday from gender, it was back to the old grind . . .

Besides, all that was years ago, of course. That was before television.

Ashputtle
or The Mother's Ghost

Three versions of one story

=====

1 THE MUTILATED GIRLS

But although you could easily take the story away from Ashputtle and centre it on the mutilated sisters – indeed, it would be easy to think of it as a story about cutting bits off women, so that they will *fit in*, some sort of circumcision-like ritual chop, nevertheless, the story always begins not with Ashputtle or her stepsisters but with Ashputtle's mother, as though it is really always the story of her mother even if, at the beginning of the story, the mother herself is just about to exit the narrative because she is at death's door: 'A rich man's wife fell sick, and, feeling that her end was near, she called her only daughter to her bedside.'

Note the absence of the husband/father. Although the woman is defined by her relation to him ('a rich man's wife') the daughter is unambiguously hers, as if hers alone, and the entire drama concerns only women, takes place almost exclusively among women, is a fight between two groups of women – in the right-hand corner, Ashputtle and her mother; in the left-hand corner, the stepmother and *her* daughters, of whom the father is unacknowledged but all the same is predicated by both textual and biological necessity.

In the drama between two female families in opposition to one another because of their rivalry over men (husband/

father, husband/son), the men seem no more than passive victims of their fancy, yet their significance is absolute because it is ('a rich man', 'a king's son') economic.

Ashputtle's father, the old man, is the first object of their desire and their dissension; the stepmother snatches him from the dead mother before her corpse is cold, as soon as her grip loosens. Then there is the young man, the potential bridegroom, the hypothetical son-in-law, for whose possession the mothers fight, using their daughters as instruments of war or as surrogates in the business of mating.

If the men, and the bank balances for which they stand, are the passive victims of the two grown women, then the girls, all three, are animated solely by the wills of their mothers. Even if Ashputtle's mother dies at the beginning of the story, her status as one of the dead only makes her position more authoritative. The mother's ghost dominates the narrative and is, in a real sense, the motive centre, the event that makes all the other events happen.

On her death bed, the mother assures the daughter: 'I shall always look after you and always be with you.' The story tells you how she does it.

At this point, when her mother makes her promise, Ashputtle is nameless. She is her mother's daughter. That is all we know. It is the stepmother who names her Ashputtle, as a joke, and, in doing so, wipes out her real name, whatever that is, banishes her from the family, exiles her from the shared table to the lonely hearth among the cinders, removes her contingent but honourable status as daughter and gives her, instead, the contingent but disreputable status of servant.

Her mother told Ashputtle she would always look after her, but then she died and the father married again and gave Ashputtle an imitation mother with daughters of her own whom she loves with the same fierce passion as

Ashputtle's mother did and still, posthumously, does, as we shall find out.

With the second marriage comes the vexed question: who shall be the daughters of the house? Mine! declares the stepmother and sets the freshly named, non-daughter Ashputtle to sweep and scrub and sleep on the hearth while her daughters lie between clean sheets in Ashputtle's bed. Ashputtle, no longer known as the daughter of her mother, nor of her father either, goes by a dry, dirty, cindery nickname for everything has turned to dust and ashes.

Meanwhile, the false mother sleeps in the bed where the real mother died and is, presumably, pleasured by the husband/father in that bed, unless there is no pleasure in it for her. We are not told what the husband/father does as regards domestic or marital function, but we can surely make the assumption that he and the stepmother share a bed, because that is what married people do.

And what can the real mother/wife do about it? Burn as she might with love, anger and jealousy, she is dead and buried.

The father, in this story, is a mystery to me. Is he so besotted with his new wife that he cannot see how his daughter is soiled with kitchen refuse and filthy from her ashy bed and always hard at work? If he sensed there was a drama in hand, he was content to leave the entire production to the women for, absent as he might be, always remember that it is in *his* house where Ashputtle sleeps on the cinders, and he is the invisible link that binds both sets of mothers and daughters in their violent equation. He is the unmoved mover, the unseen organising principle, like God, and, like God, up he pops in person, one fine day, to introduce the essential plot device.

Besides, without the absent father there would be no story because there would have been no conflict.

If they had been able to put aside their differences and discuss everything amicably, they'd have combined to expel the father. Then all the women could have slept in one bed. If they'd kept the father on, he could have done the housework.

This is the essential plot device introduced by the father: he says, 'I am about to take a business trip. What presents would my three girls like me to bring back for them?'

Note that: his *three* girls.

It occurs to me that perhaps the stepmother's daughters were really, all the time, his own daughters, just as much his own daughters as Ashputtle, his 'natural' daughters, as they say, as though there is something inherently unnatural about legitimacy. *That* would realign the forces in the story. It would make his connivance with the ascendancy of the other girls more plausible. It would make the speedy marriage, the stepmother's hostility, more probable.

But it would also transform the story into something else, because it would provide motivation, and so on; it would mean I'd have to provide a past for all these people, that I would have to equip them with three dimensions, with tastes and memories, and I would have to think of things for them to eat and wear and say. It would transform 'Ashputtle' from the bare necessity of fairy tale, with its characteristic copula formula, 'and then', to the emotional and technical complexity of bourgeois realism. They would have to learn to think. Everything would change.

I will stick with what I know.

What presents do his three girls want?

'Bring me a silk dress,' said his eldest girl. 'Bring me a string of pearls,' said the middle one. What about the third one, the forgotten one, called out of the kitchen on a charitable impulse and drying her hands, raw with housework, on her apron, bringing with her the smell of old fire?

'Bring me the first branch that knocks against your hat on the way home,' said Ashputtle.

Why did she ask for that? Did she make an informed guess at how little he valued her? Or had a dream told her to use this random formula of unacknowledged desire, to allow blind chance to choose her present for her? Unless it was her mother's ghost, awake and restlessly looking for a way home, that came into the girl's mouth and spoke the request for her.

He brought her back a hazel twig. She planted it on her mother's grave and watered it with tears. It grew into a hazel tree. When Ashputtle came out to weep upon her mother's grave, the turtle dove crooned: 'I'll never leave you, I'll always protect you.'

Then Ashputtle knew that the turtle dove was her mother's ghost and she herself was still her mother's daughter, and although she had wept and wailed and longed to have her mother back again, now her heart sank a little to find out that her mother, though dead, was no longer gone and henceforward she must do her mother's bidding.

Came the time for that curious fair they used to hold in that country, when all the resident virgins went to dance in front of the king's son so that he could pick out the girl he wanted to marry.

The turtle dove was mad for that, for her daughter to marry the prince. You might have thought her own experience of marriage might have taught her to be wary, but no, needs must, what else is a girl to do? The turtle dove was mad for her daughter to marry so she flew in and picked up the new silk dress with her beak, dragged it to the open window, threw it down to Ashputtle. She did the same with the string of pearls. Ashputtle had a good wash under the pump in the yard, put on her stolen finery and crept out the back way, secretly, to the dancing grounds, but the stepsisters had to stay home and sulk because they had nothing to wear.

The turtle dove stayed close to Ashputtle, pecking her ears to make her dance vivaciously, so that the prince would see her, so that the prince would love her, so that he would follow her and find the clue of the fallen slipper, for the story is not complete without the ritual humiliation of the other woman and the mutilation of her daughters.

The search for the foot that fits the slipper is essential to the enactment of this ritual humiliation.

The other woman wants that young man desperately. She would do anything to catch him. Not losing a daughter, but gaining a son. She wants a son so badly she is prepared to cripple her daughters. She takes up a carving knife and chops off her elder daughter's big toe, so that her foot will fit the little shoe.

Imagine.

Brandishing the carving knife, the woman bears down on her child, who is as distraught as if she had not been a girl but a boy and the old woman was after a more essential portion than a toe. 'No!' she screams. 'Mother! No! Not the knife! No!' But off it comes, all the same, and she throws it in the fire, among the ashes, where Ashputtle finds it, wonders at it, and feels both awe and fear at the phenomenon of mother love.

Mother love, which winds about these daughters like a shroud.

The prince saw nothing familiar in the face of the tearful young woman, one shoe off, one shoe on, displayed to him in triumph by her mother, but he said: 'I promised I would marry whoever the shoe fitted so I will marry you,' and they rode off together.

The turtle dove came flying round and did not croon or

coo to the bridal pair but sang a horrid song: 'Look! Look! There's blood in the shoe!'

The prince returned the ersatz ex-fiancée at once, angry at the trick, but the stepmother hastily lopped off her other daughter's heel and pushed *that* poor foot into the bloody shoe as soon as it was vacant so, nothing for it, a man of his word, the prince helped up the new girl and once again he rode away.

Back came the nagging turtle dove: 'Look!' And, sure enough, the shoe was full of blood again.

'Let Ashputtle try,' said the eager turtle dove.

So now Ashputtle must put her foot into this hideous receptacle, this open wound, still slick and warm as it is, for nothing in any of the many texts of this tale suggests the prince washed the shoe out between the fittings. It was an ordeal in itself to put a naked foot into the bloody shoe, but her mother, the turtle dove, urged her to do so in a soft, cooing croon that could not be denied.

If she does not plunge without revulsion into this open wound, she won't be fit to marry. That is the song of the turtle dove, while the other mad mother stood impotently by.

Ashputtle's foot, the size of the bound foot of a Chinese woman, a stump. Almost an amputee already, she put her tiny foot in it.

'Look! Look!' cried the turtle dove in triumph, even while the bird betrayed its ghostly nature by becoming progressively more and more immaterial as Ashputtle stood up in the shoe and commenced to walk around. Squelch, went the stump of the foot in the shoe. Squelch. 'Look!' sang out the turtle dove. 'Her foot fits the shoe like a corpse fits the coffin!

'See how well I look after you, my darling!'

2 THE BURNED CHILD

A burned child lived in the ashes. No, not really burned —
more charred, a little bit charred, like a stick half-burned
and picked off the fire. She looked like charcoal and ashes
because she lived in the ashes since her mother died and
the hot ashes burned her so she was scabbed and scarred.
The burned child lived on the hearth, covered in ashes, as
if she were still mourning.

After her mother died and was buried, her father forgot
the mother and forgot the child and married the woman
who used to rake the ashes, and that was why the child
lived in the unraked ashes, and there was nobody to brush
her hair, so it stuck out like a mat, nor to wipe the dirt off
her scabbed face, and she had no heart to do it for herself,
but she raked the ashes and slept beside the little cat and
got the burned bits from the bottom of the pot to eat,
scraping them out, squatting on the floor, by herself in
front of the fire, not as if she were human, because she was
still mourning.

Her mother was dead and buried, but felt perfect exquis-
ite pain of love when she looked up through the earth and
saw the burned child covered in ashes.

'Milk the cow, burned child, and bring back all the milk,'
said the stepmother, who used to rake the ashes and milk
the cow, once upon a time, but the burned child did all
that, now.

The ghost of the mother went into the cow.

'Drink milk, grow fat,' said the mother's ghost.

The burned child pulled on the udder and drank enough
milk before she took the bucket back and nobody saw, and
time passed, she drank milk every day, she grew fat, she
grew breasts, she grew up.

There was a man the stepmother wanted and she asked

him into the kitchen to get his dinner, but she made the burned child cook it, although the stepmother did all the cooking before. After the burned child cooked the dinner the stepmother sent her off to milk the cow.

'I want that man for myself,' said the burned child to the cow.

The cow let down more milk, and more, and more, enough for the girl to have a drink and wash her face and wash her hands. When she washed her face, she washed the scabs off and now she was not burned at all, but the cow was empty.

'Give your own milk, next time,' said the ghost of the mother inside the cow. 'You've milked me dry.'

The little cat came by. The ghost of the mother went into the cat.

'Your hair wants doing,' said the cat. 'Lie down.'

The little cat unpicked her raggy lugs with its clever paws until the burned child's hair hung down nicely, but it had been so snagged and tangled that the cat's claws were all pulled out before it was finished.

'Comb your own hair, next time,' said the cat. 'You've maimed me.'

The burned child was clean and combed, but stark naked.

There was a bird sitting in the apple tree. The ghost of the mother left the cat and went into the bird. The bird struck its own breast with its beak. Blood poured down on to the burned child under the tree. It ran over her shoulders and covered her front and covered her back. When the bird had no more blood, the burned child got a red silk dress.

'Make your own dress, next time,' said the bird. 'I'm through with that bloody business.'

The burned child went into the kitchen to show herself to the man. She was not burned any more, but lovely. The man left off looking at the stepmother and looked at the girl.

'Come home with me and let your stepmother stay and rake the ashes,' he said to her and off they went. He gave her a house and money. She did all right.

'Now I can go to sleep,' said the ghost of the mother. 'Now everything is all right.'

3 TRAVELLING CLOTHES

The stepmother took the red-hot poker and burned the orphan's face with it because she had not raked the ashes. The girl went to her mother's grave. In the earth her mother said: 'It must be raining. Or else it is snowing. Unless there is a heavy dew tonight.'

'It isn't raining, it isn't snowing, it's too early for the dew. My tears are falling on your grave, mother.'

The dead woman waited until night came. Then she climbed out and went to the house. The stepmother slept on a feather bed, but the burned child slept on the hearth among the ashes. When the dead woman kissed her, the scar vanished. The girl woke up. The dead woman gave her a red dress.

'I had it when I was your age.'

The girl put the red dress on. The dead woman took worms from her eyesockets; they turned into jewels. The girl put on a diamond ring.

'I had it when I was your age.'

They went together to the grave.

'Step into my coffin.'

'No,' said the girl. She shuddered.

'I stepped into *my* mother's coffin when I was your age.'

The girl stepped into the coffin although she thought it

would be the death of her. It turned into a coach and horses. The horses stamped, eager to be gone.

'Go and seek your fortune, darling.'

Alice in Prague
or The Curious Room

———

This piece was written in praise of Jan Svankmayer,
the animator of Prague, and his film of *Alice*

In the city of Prague, once, it was winter.

Outside the curious room, there is a sign on the door which
says 'Forbidden'. Inside, inside, oh, come and see! The
celebrated DR DEE.

The celebrated Dr Dee, looking for all the world like
Santa Claus on account of his long, white beard and apple
cheeks, is contemplating his crystal, the fearful sphere that
contains everything that is, or was, or ever shall be.

It is a round ball of solid glass and gives a deceptive
impression of weightlessness, because you can see right
through it and we falsely assume an equation between light-
ness and transparency, that what the light shines through
cannot be there and so must weigh nothing. In fact, the
Doctor's crystal ball is heavy enough to inflict a substantial
injury and the Doctor's assistant, Ned Kelly, the Man in
the Iron Mask, often weighs the ball in one hand or tosses
it back and forth from one to the other hand as he ponders
the fragility of the hollow bone, his master's skull, as it
pores heedless over some tome.

Ned Kelly would blame the murder on the angels. He

would say the angels came out of the sphere. Everybody knows the angels live there.

The crystal resembles: an aqueous humour, frozen;

a glass eye, although without any iris or pupil – just the sort of transparent eye, in fact, which the adept might construe as apt to see the invisible;

a tear, round, as it forms within the eye, for a tear acquires its characteristic shape of a pear, what we think of as a 'tear' shape, only in the act of falling;

the shining drop that trembles, sometimes, on the tip of the Doctor's well-nigh senescent, tending towards the flaccid, yet nevertheless sustainable and discernible morning erection, and always reminds him of

a drop of dew,

a drop of dew endlessly, tremulously about to fall from the unfolded petals of a rose and, therefore, like the tear, retaining the perfection of its circumference only by refusing to sustain free fall, remaining

what it is, because it refuses to
become what it might be, the
antithesis of metamorphosis;

and yet, in old England, far away,
the sign of the Do Drop Inn will
always, that jovial pun, show an
oblate spheroid, heavily
tinselled, because the sign-
painter, in order to demonstrate
the idea of 'drop', needs must
represent the dew in the act of
falling and therefore, for the
purposes of this comparison,
not resembling the numinous ball
weighing down the angelic
Doctor's outstretched palm.

For Dr Dee, the invisible is only another unexplored
country, a brave new world.

The hinge of the sixteenth century, where it joins with
the seventeenth century, is as creaky and judders open as
reluctantly as the door in a haunted house. Through that
door, in the distance, we may glimpse the distant light of
the Age of Reason, but precious little of that is about to
fall on Prague, the capital of paranoia, where the fortune-
tellers live on Golden Alley in cottages so small, a good-
sized doll would find itself cramped, and there is one certain
house on Alchemist's Street that only becomes visible
during a thick fog. (On sunny days, you see a stone.) But,
even in the fog, only those born on the Sabbath can see the
house anyway.

Like a lamp guttering out in a recently vacated room, the Renaissance flared, faded and extinguished itself. The world had suddenly revealed itself as bewilderingly infinite, but since the imagination remained, for after all it is only human, finite, our imaginations took some time to catch up. If Francis Bacon will die in 1626 a martyr to experimental science, having contracted a chill whilst stuffing a dead hen with snow on Highgate Hill to see if that would keep it fresh, in Prague, where Dr Faustus once lodged in Charles Square, Dr Dee, the English expatriate alchemist, awaits the manifestation of the angel in the Archduke Rudolph's curious room, and we are still fumbling our way towards the end of the previous century.

The Archduke Rudolph keeps his priceless collection of treasures in this curious room; he numbers the Doctor amongst these treasures and is therefore forced to number the Doctor's assistant, the unspeakable and iron-visaged Kelly, too.

The Archduke Rudolph has crazy eyes. These eyes are the mirrors of his soul.

It is very cold this afternoon, the kind of weather that makes a person piss. The moon is up already, a moon the colour of candlewax and, as the sky discolours when the night comes on, the moon grows more white, more cold, white as the source of all the cold in the world, until, when the winter moon reaches its chill meridian, everything will freeze – not only the water in the jug and the ink in the well, but the blood in the vein, the aqueous humour.

Metamorphosis.

In their higgledy-piggledy disorder, the twigs on the bare

trees outside the thick window resemble those random scratchings made by common use that you only see when you lift your wineglass up to the light. A hard frost has crisped the surface of the deep snow on the Archduke's tumbled roofs and turrets. In the snow, a raven: caw!

Dr Dee knows the language of birds and sometimes speaks it, but what the birds say is frequently banal; all the raven said, over and over, was: 'Poor Tom's a-cold!'

Above the Doctor's head, slung from the low-beamed ceiling, dangles a flying turtle, stuffed. In the dim room we can make out, amongst much else, the random juxtaposition of an umbrella, a sewing machine and a dissecting table; a raven and a writing desk; an aged mermaid, poor wizened creature, cramped in a foetal position in a jar, her ream of grey hair suspended adrift in the viscous liquid that preserves her, her features rendered greenish and somewhat distorted by the flaws in the glass.

Dr Dee would like, for a mate to this mermaid, to keep in a cage, if alive, or, if dead, in a stoppered bottle, an angel.

It was an age in love with wonders.

Dr Dee's assistant, Ned Kelly, the Man in the Iron Mask, is also looking for angels. He is gazing at the sheeny, reflective screen of his scrying disc which is made of polished coal. The angels visit him more frequently than they do the Doctor, but, for some reason, Dr Dee cannot see Kelly's guests, although they crowd the surface of the scrying disc, crying out in their high, piercing voices in the species of bird-creole with which they communicate. It is a great sadness to him.

Kelly, however, is phenomenally gifted in this direction and notes down on a pad the intonations of their speech which, though he doesn't understand it himself, the Doctor excitedly makes sense of.

But, today, no go.

Kelly yawns. He stretches. He feels the pressure of the weather on his bladder.

The privy at the top of the tower is a hole in the floor behind a cupboard door. It is situated above another privy, with another hole, above another privy, another hole, and so on, down seven further privies, seven more holes, until your excreta at last hurtles into the cesspit far below. The cold keeps the smell down, thank God.

Dr Dee, ever the seeker after knowledge, has calculated the velocity of a flying turd.

Although a man could hang himself in the privy with ease and comfort, securing the rope about the beam above and launching himself into the void to let gravity break his neck for him, Kelly, whether at stool or making water, never allows the privy to remind him of the 'long drop' nor even, however briefly, admires his own instrument for fear the phrase 'well-hung' recalls the noose which he narrowly escaped in his native England for fraud, once, in Lancaster; for forgery, once, in Rutlandshire; and for performing a confidence trick in Ashby-de-la-Zouch.

But his ears were cropped for him in the pillory at Walton-le-Dale, after he dug up a corpse from a churchyard for purposes of necromancy, or possibly of grave-robbing, and this is why, in order to conceal this amputation, he always wears the iron mask modelled after that which will be worn by a namesake three hundred years hence in a country that does not yet exist, an iron mask like an upturned bucket with a slit cut for his eyes.

Kelly, unbuttoning, wonders if his piss will freeze in the

act of falling; if, today, it is cold enough in Prague to let him piss an arc of ice.

No.

He buttons up again.

Women loathe this privy. Happily, few venture here, into the magician's tower, where the Archduke Rudolph keeps his collection of wonders, his proto-museum, his '*Wunder-kammer*', his '*cabinet de curiosités*', that *curious room* of which he speak.

There's a theory, one I find persuasive, that the quest for knowledge is, at bottom, the search for the answer to the question: 'Where was I before I was born?'

In the beginning was . . . what?

Perhaps, in the beginning, there was a curious room, a room like this one, crammed with wonders; and now the room and all it contains are forbidden you, although it was made just for you, had been prepared for you since time began, and you will spend all your life trying to remember it.

Kelly once took the Archduke aside and offered him, at a price, a little piece of the beginning, a slice of the fruit of the Tree of the Knowledge of Good and Evil itself, which Kelly claimed he had obtained from an Armenian, who had found it on Mount Ararat, growing in the shadows of the wreck of the Ark. The slice had dried out with time and looked very much like a dehydrated ear.

The Archduke soon decided it was a fake, that Kelly had been fooled. The Archduke is *not* gullible. Rather, he has a boundless desire to know *everything* and an exceptional generosity of belief. At night, he stands on top of the tower and watches the stars in the company of Tycho Brahe and Johann Kepler, yet by day, he makes no move nor judgement before he consults the astrologers in their zodiacal hats and yet, in those days, either an astrologer or an astronomer would be hard put to it to describe the difference between their disciplines.

He is not gullible. But he has his peculiarities.

The Archduke keeps a lion chained up in his bedroom as a species of watch-dog or, since the lion is a member of the *Felis* family and not a member of the *Cave canem* family, a giant guard-cat. For fear of the lion's yellow teeth, the Archduke had them pulled. Now that the poor beast cannot chew, he must subsist on slop. The lion lies with his head on his paws, dreaming. If you could open up his brain this moment, you would find nothing there but the image of a beefsteak.

Meanwhile, the Archduke, in the curtained privacy of his bed, embraces something, God knows what.

Whatever it is, he does it with such energy that the bell hanging over the bed becomes agitated due to the jolting and rhythmic lurching of the bed, and the clapper jangles against the sides.

Ting-a-ling!

The bell is cast out of *electrum magicum*. Paracelsus said that a bell cast out of *electrum magicum* would summon up the spirits. If a rat gnaws the Archduke's toe during the night, his involuntary start will agitate the bell immediately so the spirits can come and chase the rat away, for the lion, although *sui generis* a cat is not sufficiently a cat in spirit to perform the domestic functions of a common mouser, not like the little calico beastie who keeps the good Doctor company and often, out of pure affection, brings him furry tributes of those she has slain.

Though the bell rings, softly at first, and then with increasing fury as the Archduke nears the end of his journey, no spirits come. But there have been no rats either.

A split fig falls out of the bed on to the marble floor with a soft, exhausted plop, followed by a hand of bananas, that spread out and go limp, as if in submission.

'Why can't he make do with meat, like other people,' whined the hungry lion.

Can the Archduke be effecting intercourse with a fruit salad?

Or with Carmen Miranda's hat?

Worse.

The hand of bananas indicates the Archduke's enthusiasm for the newly discovered Americas. Oh, brave new world! There is a street in Prague called 'New World' (*Novy Svet*). The hand of bananas is freshly arrived from Bermuda via his Spanish kin, who know what he likes. He has a particular enthusiasm for weird plants, and every week comes to converse with his mandrakes, those warty, shaggy roots that originate (the Archduke shudders pleasurably to think about it) in the sperm and water spilled by a hanged man.

The mandrakes live at ease in a special cabinet. It falls to Ned Kelly's reluctant duty to bathe each of these roots once a week in milk and dress them up in fresh linen nightgowns. Kelly, reluctantly, since the roots, warts and all, resemble so many virile members, and he does not like to handle them, imagining they raucously mock his manhood as he tends them, believing they unman him.

The Archduke's collection also boasts some magnificent specimens of the *coco-de-mer*, or double coconut, which grows in the shape, but exactly the shape, of the pelvic area of a woman, a foot long, heft and clefted, I kid you not. The Archduke and his gardeners plan to effect a vegetable marriage and will raise the progeny – *man-de-mer* or *coco-drake* – in his own greenhouses. (The Archduke himself is a confirmed bachelor.)

The bell ceases. The lion sighs with relief and lays his head once more upon his heavy paws: 'Now I can sleep!'

Then, from under the bed curtains, on either side of the bed, begins to pour a veritable torrent that quickly forms into dark, viscous, livid puddles on the floor.

But, before you accuse the Archduke of the unspeakable, dip your finger in the puddle and lick it.

Delicious!

For these are sticky puddles of freshly squeezed grape juice, and apple juice, and peach juice, juice of plum, pear, or raspberry, strawberry, cherry ripe, blackberry, black currant, white currant, red . . . The room brims with the delicious ripe scent of summer pudding, even though, outside, on the frozen tower, the crow still creaks out his melancholy call:

'Poor Tom's a-cold!'

And it is midwinter.

Night was. Widow Night, an old woman in mourning, with big, black wings, came beating against the window; they kept her out with lamps and candles.

When he went back into the laboratory, Ned Kelly found that Dr Dee had nodded off to sleep as the old man often did nowadays towards the end of the day, the crystal ball having rolled from palm to lap as he lay back in the black oak chair, and now, as he shifted at the impulse of a dream, it rolled again off his lap, down on to the floor, where it landed with a soft thump on the rushes – no harm done – and the little calico cat disabled it at once with a swift blow of her right paw, then began to play with it, batting it that way and this before she administered the *coup de grâce*.

With a gusty sigh, Kelly once more addressed his scrying disc, although today he felt barren of invention. He reflected ironically that, if just so much as one wee feathery angel ever, even the one time, should escape the scrying disc and flutter into the laboratory, the cat would surely get it.

Not, Kelly knew, that such a thing was possible.

If you could see inside Kelly's brain, you would discover a calculating machine.

Widow Night painted the windows black.

Then, all at once, the cat made a noise like sharply crumpled paper, a noise of enquiry and concern. A rat? Kelly turned to look. The cat, head on one side, was considering, with such scrupulous intensity that its pricked ears met at the tips, something lying on the floor beside the crystal ball, so that at first it looked as if the glass eye had shed a tear.

But look again.

Kelly looked again and began to sob and gibber.

The cat rose up and backed away all in one liquid motion, hissing, its bristling tail stuck straight up, stiff as a broom handle, too scared to permit even the impulse of attack upon the creature, about the size of a little finger, that popped out of the crystal ball as if the ball had been a bubble.

But its passage has not cracked or fissured the ball; it is still whole, has sealed itself up again directly after the departure of the infinitesimal child who, so suddenly released from her sudden confinement, now experimentally stretches out her tiny limbs to test the limits of the new invisible circumference around her.

Kelly stammered: 'There must be some rational explanation!'

Although they were too small for him to see them, her teeth still had the transparency and notched edges of the first stage of the second set; her straight, fair hair was cut in a stern fringe; she scowled and sat upright, looking about her with evident disapproval.

The cat, cowering ecstatically, now knocked over an alembic and a quantity of *elixir vitae* ran away through the rushes. At the bang, the Doctor woke and was not astonished to see her.

He bade her a graceful welcome in the language of the tawny pippit.

How did she get there?

She was kneeling on the mantelpiece of the sitting room of the place she lived, looking at herself in the mirror. Bored, she breathed on the glass until it clouded over and then, with her finger, she drew a door. The door opened. She sprang through and, after a brief moment's confusing fish-eye view of a vast, gloomy chamber, scarcely illuminated by five candles in one branched stick and filled with all the clutter in the world, her view was obliterated by the clawed paw of a vast cat extended ready to strike, hideously increasing in size as it approached her, and then, splat! she burst out of 'time will be' into 'time was', for the transparent substance which surrounded her burst like a bubble and there she was, in her pink frock, lying on some rushes under the gaze of a tender ancient with a long, white beard and a man with a coal-scuttle on his head.

Her lips moved but no sound came out; she had left her voice behind in the mirror. She flew into a tantrum and beat her heels upon the floor, weeping furiously. The Doctor, who, in some remote time past, raised children of his own, let her alone until, her passion spent, she heaved and grunted on the rushes, knuckling her eyes; then he peered into the depths of a big china bowl on a dim shelf and produced from out of it a strawberry.

The child accepted the strawberry suspiciously, for it was, although not large, the size of her head. She sniffed it, turned it round and round, and then essayed just one little bite out of it, leaving behind a tiny ring of white within the crimson flesh. Her teeth were perfect.

At the first bite, she grew a little.

Kelly continued to mumble: 'There must be some rational explanation.'

The child took a second, less tentative bite, and grew a little more. The mandrakes in their white nightgowns woke up and began to mutter among themselves.

Reassured at last, she gobbled the strawberry all up, but she had been falsely reassured; now her flaxen crown bumped abruptly against the rafters, out of the range of the candlestick so they could not see her face but a gigantic tear splashed with a metallic clang upon Ned Kelly's helmet, then another, and the Doctor, with some presence of mind, before they needed to hurriedly construct an Ark, pressed a phial of *elixir vitae* into her hand. When she drank it, she shrank down again until soon she was small enough to sit on his knee, her blue eyes staring with wonder at his beard, as white as ice-cream and as long as Sunday.

But she had no wings.

Kelly, the faker, knew there *must* be a rational explanation but he could not think of one.

*

She found her voice at last.

'Tell me,' she said, 'the answer to this problem: the Governor of Kgoujni wants to give a very small dinner party, and invites his father's brother-in-law, his brother's father-in-law, his father-in-law's brother, and his brother-in-law's father. Find the number of guests.'[1]

At the sound of her voice, which was as clear as a looking-glass, everything in the curious room gave a shake and a shudder and, for a moment, looked as if it were painted on gauze, like a theatrical effect, and might disappear if a bright light were shone on it. Dr Dee stroked his beard reflectively. He could provide answers to many questions, or knew where to look for answers. He had gone and caught a falling starre – didn't a piece of it lie beside the stuffed dodo? To impregnate the aggressively phallic mandrake, with its masculinity to the power of two, as implied by its name, was a task which, he pondered, the omnivorous Archduke, with his enthusiasm for erotic esoterica, might prove capable of. And the answer to the other two imponderables posed by the poet were obtainable, surely, through the intermediary of the angels, if only one scried long enough.

He truly believed that nothing was unknowable. That is what makes him modern.

But, to the child's question, he can imagine no answer.

Kelly, forced against his nature to suspect the presence of another world that would destroy his confidence in tricks, is sunk in introspection, and has not even heard her.

However, such magic as there is in *this* world, as opposed to the worlds that can be made out of dictionaries, can only be real when it is artificial and Dr Dee himself, whilst a member of the Cambridge Footlights at university, before his beard was white or long, directed a famous production of Aristophanes' *Peace* at Trinity College, in which he sent a grocer's boy right up to heaven, laden with his basket as if to make deliveries, on the back of a giant beetle.

Archytas made a flying dove of wood. At Nuremberg, according to Boterus, an adept constructed both an eagle and a fly and set them to flutter and flap across his laboratory, to the astonishment of all. In olden times, the statues that Daedalus built raised their arms and moved their legs due to the action of weights, and of shifting deposits of mercury. Albertus Magnus, the Great Sage, cast a head in brass that spoke.

Are they animate or not, these beings that jerk and shudder into such a semblance of life? Do these creatures believe themselves to be human? And if they do, at what point might they, by virtue of the sheer intensity of their belief, become so?

(In Prague, the city of the Golem, an image can come to life.)

The Doctor thinks about these things a great deal and thinks the child upon his knee, babbling about the inhabitants of another world, must be a little automaton popped up from God knows where.

Meanwhile, the door marked 'Forbidden' opened up again.

It came in.

It rolled on little wheels, a wobbling, halting, toppling progress, a clockwork land galleon, tall as a mast, advancing at a stately if erratic pace, nodding and becking and shedding inessential fragments of its surface as it came, its foliage rustling, now stuck and perilously rocking at a crack in the stone floor with which its wheels cannot cope, now flying helter-skelter, almost out of control, wobbling, clicking, whirring, an eclectic juggernaut evidently almost on the point of collapse; it has been a heavy afternoon.

But, although it looked as if eccentrically self-propelled, Arcimboldo the Milanese pushed it, picking up bits of the thing as they fell off, tut-tutting at its ruination, pushing it, shoving it, occasionally picking it up bodily and carrying it. He was smeared all over with its secretions and looked forward to a good wash once it had been returned to the curious room from whence it came. There, the Doctor and his assistant will take it apart until the next time.

This thing before us, although it is not, was not and never will be alive, *has* been animate and will be animate again, but, at the moment, not, for now, after one final shove, it stuck stock still, wheels halted, wound down, uttering one last, gross, mechanical sigh.

A nipple dropped off. The Doctor picked it up and offered it to the child. Another strawberry! She shook her head.

The size and prominence of the secondary sexual characteristics indicate this creature is, like the child, of the feminine gender. She lives in the fruit bowl where the Doctor found the first strawberry. When the Archduke wants her, Arcimboldo, who designed her, puts her together again, arranging the fruit of which she is composed on a wicker frame, always a little different from the last time according to what the greenhouse can provide. Today, her hair is largely composed of green muscat grapes, her nose a pear, eyes filbert nuts, cheeks russet apples somewhat wrinkled – never mind! The Archduke has a penchant for older women. When the painter got her ready, she looked like Carmen Miranda's hat on wheels, but her name was 'Summer'.

But now, what devastation! Hair mashed, nose squashed,

bosom puréed, belly juiced. The child observed this apparition with the greatest interest. She spoke again. She queried earnestly:

'If 70 per cent have lost an eye, 75 per cent an ear, 80 per cent an arm, 85 per cent a leg: what percentage, *at least*, must have lost all four?'[2]

Once again, she stumped them. They pondered, all three men, and at last slowly shook their heads. As if the child's question were the last straw, 'Summer' now disintegrated – subsided, slithered, slopped off her frame into her fruit bowl, whilst shed fruit, some almost whole, bounced to the rushes around her. The Milanese, with a pang, watched his design disintegrate.

It is not so much that the Archduke likes to pretend this monstrous being is alive, for nothing inhuman is alien to him; rather, he does not care whether she is alive or no, that what he wants to do is to plunge his member into her artificial strangeness, perhaps as he does so imagining himself an orchard and this embrace, this plunge into the succulent flesh, which is not flesh as we know it, which is, if you like, the living metaphor – '*fica*' – explains Arcimboldo, displaying the orifice – this intercourse with the very flesh of summer will fructify his cold kingdom, the snowy country outside the window, where the creaking raven endlessly laments the inclement weather.

'Reason becomes the enemy which withholds from us so many possibilities of pleasure,' said Freud.

One day, when the fish within the river freeze, the day of the frigid lunar noon, the Archduke will come to Dr Dee, his crazy eyes resembling, the one, a blackberry, the other, a cherry, and say: transform me into a harvest festival!

So he did; but the weather got no better.

*

Peckish, Kelly absently demolished a fallen peach, so lost in thought he never noticed the purple bruise, and the little cat played croquet with the peach stone while Dr Dee, stirred by memories of his English children long ago and far away, stroked the girl's flaxen hair.

'Whither comest thou?' he asked her.

The question stirred her again into speech.

'A and B began the year with only £1,000 apiece,' she announced, urgently.

The three men turned to look at her as if she were about to pronounce some piece of oracular wisdom. She tossed her blonde head. She went on.

'They borrowed nought; they stole nought. On the next New Year's Day they had £60,000 between them. How did they do it?'[3]

They could not think of a reply. They continued to stare at her, words turning to dust in their mouths.

'How did they do it?' she repeated, now almost with desperation, as if, if they only could stumble on the correct reply, she would be precipitated back, diminutive, stern, rational, within the crystal ball and thence be tossed back through the mirror to 'time will be', or, even better, to the book from which she had sprung.

'Poor Tom's a-cold,' offered the raven. After that, came silence.

Note

The answers to Alice's conundrums:

1 One.

2 Ten.

3 They went that day to the Bank of England. A stood in front of it, while B went round and stood behind it.

Problems and answers from *A Tangled Tale*, Lewis Carroll,
London, 1885.

Alice was invented by a logician and therefore she comes
from the world of nonsense, that is, from the world of
non-sense – the opposite of common sense; this world is
constructed by logical deduction and is created by language,
although language shivers into abstractions within it.

Impressions: The Wrightsman Magdalene

For a woman to be a virgin and a mother, you need a miracle; when a woman is not a virgin, nor a mother, either, nobody talks about miracles. Mary, the mother of Jesus, together with the other Mary, the mother of St John, and the Mary Magdalene, the repentant harlot, went down to the seashore; a woman named Fatima, a servant, went with them. They stepped into a boat, they threw away the rudder, they permitted the sea to take them where it wanted. It beached them near Marseilles.

Don't run away with the idea the South of France was an easy option compared to the deserts of Syria, or Egypt, or the wastes of Cappadocia, where other early saints, likewise driven by the imperious need for solitude, found arid, inhospitable crevices in which to contemplate the ineffable. There were clean, square, white, Roman cities all along the Mediterranean coast everywhere except the place the three Marys landed with their servant. They landed in the middle of a malarial swamp, the Camargue. It was not pleasant. The desert would have been more healthy.

But there the two stern mothers and Fatima – don't forget Fatima – set up a chapel, at the place we now call Saintes-Maries-de-la-Mer. There they stayed. But the other Mary, the Magdalene, the not-mother, could not stop. Impelled by the demon of loneliness, she went off on her own through the Camargue; then she crossed limestone hill after limestone hill. Flints cut her feet, sun burned her skin.

She ate fruit that had fallen from the tree of its own accord, like a perfect Manichean. She ate dropped berries. The black-browed Palestinian woman walked in silence, gaunt as famine, hairy as a dog.

She walked until she came to the forest of the Sainte-Baume. She walked until she came to the remotest part of the forest. There she found a cave. There she stopped. There she prayed. She did not speak to another human being, she did not see another human being, for thirty-three years. By then, she was old.

Mary Magdalene, the Venus in sackcloth. Georges de La Tour's picture does not show a woman in sackcloth, but her chemise is coarse and simple enough to be a penitential garment, or, at least, the kind of garment that shows you were not thinking of personal adornment when you put it on. Even though the chemise is deeply open on the bosom, it does not seem to disclose flesh as such, but a flesh that has more akin to the wax of the burning candle, to the way the wax candle is irradiated by its own flame, and glows. So you could say that, from the waist up, this Mary Magdalene is on the high road to penitence, but, from the waist down, which is always the more problematic part, there is the question of her long, red skirt.

Left-over finery? Was it the only frock she had, the frock she went whoring in, then repented in, then set sail in? Did she walk all the way to the Sainte-Baume in this red skirt? It doesn't look travel-stained or worn or torn. It is a luxurious, even a scandalous skirt. A scarlet dress for a scarlet woman.

The Virgin Mary wears blue. Her preference has sanctified the colours. We think of a 'heavenly' blue. But Mary Magdalene wears red, the colour of passion. The two women are twin paradoxes. One is not what the other is. One is a virgin and a mother; the other is a non-virgin, and childless. Note how the English language doesn't contain a specific word to describe a woman who is grown-up, sexually mature and *not* a mother, unless such a woman is using her sexuality as her profession.

Because Mary Magdalene is a woman and childless she goes out into the wilderness. The others, the mothers, stay and make a church, where people come.

But why has she taken her pearl necklace with her? Look at it, lying in front of the mirror. And her long hair has been most beautifully brushed. Is she, yet, fully repentant?

In Georges de La Tour's painting, the Magdalene's hair is well brushed. Sometimes the Magdalene's hair is as shaggy as a Rastafarian's. Sometimes her hair hangs down upon, is inextricably mixed up with, her furs. Mary Magdalene is easier to read when she is hairy, when, in the wilderness, she wears the rough coat of her own desires, as if the desires of her past have turned into the hairy shirt that torments her present, repentant flesh.

Sometimes she wears only her hair; it never saw a comb, long, matted, unkempt, hanging down to her knees. She belts her own hair round her waist with the rope with which, each night, she lashes herself, making a rough tunic of it. On these occasions, the transformation from the young, lovely, voluptuous Mary Magdalene, the happy non-virgin, the party girl, the woman taken in adultery — on these occasions, the transformation is complete. She has turned into something wild and strange, into a female version of John the Baptist, a hairy hermit, as good as naked, transcending gender, sex obliterated, nakedness irrelevant.

Now she is one with such pole-sitters as Simeon Stylites,

and other solitary cave-dwellers who communed with beasts, like St Jerome. She eats herbs, drinks water from the pool; she comes to resemble an even earlier incarnation of the 'wild man of the woods' than John the Baptist. Now she looks like hairy Enkidu, from the Babylonian *Epic of Gilgamesh*. The woman who once, in her grand, red dress, was vice personified, has now retired to an existential situation in which vice simply is not possible. She has arrived at the radiant, enlightened sinlessness of the animals. In her new, resplendent animality, she is now beyond choice. Now she has no option but virtue.

But there is another way of looking at it. Think of Donatello's Magdalene, in Florence – she's dried up by the suns of the wilderness, battered by wind and rain, anorexic, toothless, a body entirely annihilated by the soul. You can almost smell the odour of the kind of sanctity that reeks from her – it's rank, it's raw, it's horrible. By the ardour with which she has embraced the rigorous asceticism of penitence, you can tell how much she hated her early life of so-called 'pleasure'. The mortification of the flesh comes naturally to her. When you learn that Donatello intended the piece to be not black but gilded, that does not lighten its mood.

Nevertheless, you can see the point that some anonymous Man of the Enlightenment on the Grand Tour made two hundred years ago – how Donatello's Mary Magdalene made him 'disgusted with penitence'.

Penitence becomes sado-masochism. Self-punishment is its own reward.

But it can also become kitsch. Consider the apocryphal story of Mary of Egypt. Who was a beautiful prostitute until she repented and spent the remaining forty-seven years of her life as a penitent in the desert, clothed only in her long hair. She took with her three loaves and ate a mouthful of bread once a day, in the mornings; the loaves lasted her out. Mary of Egypt is clean and fresh. Her face stays miraculously unlined. She is as untouched by time as her bread is untouched by appetite. She sits on a rock in the desert, combing out her long hair, like a lorelei whose water has turned to sand. We can imagine how she smiles. Perhaps she sings a little song.

Georges de La Tour's Mary Magdalene has not yet arrived at an ecstasy of repentance, evidently. Perhaps, indeed, he has pictured her as she is just about to repent – before her sea voyage in fact, although I would prefer to think that this bare, bleak space, furnished only with the mirror, is that of her cave in the woods. But this is a woman who is still taking care of herself. Her long, black hair, sleek as that of a Japanese woman on a painted scroll – she must just have finished brushing it, reminding us that she is the patron saint of hairdressers. Her hair is the product of culture, not left as nature intended. Her hair shows she has just used the mirror as an instrument of worldly vanity. Her hair shows that, even as she meditates upon the candle flame, *this* world still has a claim upon her.

Unless we are actually watching her as her soul is drawn out into the candle flame.

We meet Mary Magdalene in the gospels, doing something extraordinary with her hair. After she massaged Jesus' feet with her pot of precious ointment, she wiped them clean with her hair, an image so astonishing and erotically precise it is surprising it is represented so rarely in art, especially that of the seventeenth century, when religious excess and eroticism went so often together. Magdalene, using her hair, that beautiful net with which she used to snare men as – well, as a mop, a washcloth, a towel. And a slight element of the perverse about it, too. All in all, the kind of *gaudy gesture* a repentant prostitute *would* make.

She has brushed her hair, perhaps for the last time, and taken off her pearl necklace, also for the last time. Now she is gazing at the candle flame, which doubles itself in the mirror. Once upon a time, that mirror was the tool of her trade; it was within the mirror that she assembled all the elements of the femininity she put together for sale. But now, instead of reflecting her face, it duplicates the pure flame.

When I was in labour, I thought of a candle flame. I was in labour for nineteen hours. At first the pains came slowly and were relatively light; it was easy to ride them. But when they came more closely together, and grew more and more intense, then I began to concentrate my mind upon an imaginary candle flame.

Look at the candle flame as if it is the only thing in the world. How white and steady it is. At the core of the white flame is a cone of blue, transparent air; that is the thing to look at, that is the thing to concentrate on. When the pains came thick and fast, I fixed all my attention on the blue absence at the heart of the flame, as though it were the secret of the flame and, if I concentrated enough upon it, it would become *my* secret, too.

Soon there was no time to think of anything else. By then, I was entirely subsumed by the blue space. Even when they snipped away at my body, down below, to finally let the baby out the easiest way, all my attention was concentrated on the core of the flame.

Once the candle flame had done its work, it snuffed itself out; they wrapped my baby in a shawl and gave him to me.

Mary Magdalene meditates upon the candle flame. She enters the blue core, the blue absence. She becomes something other than herself.

The silence in the picture, for it is the most silent of pictures, emanates not from the darkness behind the candle in the mirror but from those two candles, the real candle and the mirror candle. Between them, the two candles disseminate light and silence. They have tranced the woman into enlightenment. She can't speak, won't speak. In the desert, she will grunt, maybe, but she will put speech aside, after this, after she has meditated upon the candle flame and the mirror. She will put speech aside just as she has put aside her pearl necklace and will put away her red skirt. The new person, the saint, is being born out of this intercourse with the candle flame.

But something has already been born out of this intercourse with the candle flame. See. She carries it already. She carries where, if she were a Virgin mother and not a sacred whore, she would rest her baby, not a living child but a *memento mori*, a skull.